The Tired Canary

The Slater Ibáñez Books

That First Heady Burn
True Vermilion
The Dark Shill
A Stack of Sawbucks
The Hillside Roble
The Peroxide Pomp
The Incidental Twin
Brawl in Bardo
The Window-Shade Job
The Convenient Patsy
The Artisanal Grifter
Shrink in the Shadows
Project Chartreuse
From a Desert Playa
The Tired Canary
A Desperate Frame-up
Trail of the Blue Agave
The Saucer-Heads
The Satin Squeeze Play
Chiseler in Jade
The Eagle and the Weasel
The Mojave Gimmick
The Hapless Gonif

Subscribe to the Slater
Ibáñez Books newsletter:

slaternews.dagmarmiura.com

The Tired Canary

The Tired Canary

George Bixley

DAGMAR MIURA

LOS ANGELES

Published by Dagmar Miura
Los Angeles
www.dagmarmiura.com

The Tired Canary

This is a work of fiction. Names, characters, businesses, places, events,
and incidents are either the products of the author's imagination or
used in a fictitious manner. Any resemblance to actual persons, living
or dead, or actual events is purely coincidental.

First published 2022

ISBN: 978-1-956744-38-5

ONE

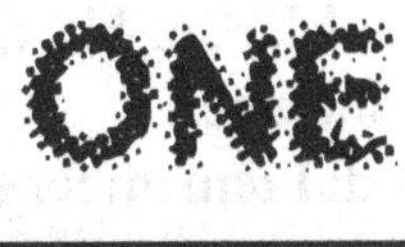

"WE'RE IN THE SAME field," Chila said, holding Slater's gaze. "I was told you know how to get things done."

They'd just sat down at his desk, across from each other, and he studied her for a moment. Her dark hair was tied back, and she wore a light nylon jacket even though it was a warm evening.

"Why come over here? Why didn't you summon me to your office?" Slater picked up her business card from his desktop. "Westside Title Guarantee. I've never heard of it."

"I actually wanted to hire you on a private matter," she said. "Not through the company."

"Your card says Isidra." He set it on the desktop. "You just said your name is Chila."

"It's a nickname. Like how Lupe is short for Guadalupe."

"I'll have to take your word for it," Slater said. "I

don't actually speak Spanish."

"You look like you should."

"I get that a lot," he said, and scowled. He had his father's dark Latin coloring, his thick black hair. "How did you hear about me?"

"Marisol Russo."

"I don't know that name."

"She used to be Marisol Hart," Chila said, "but she married someone else."

That name, he did remember—she'd hired him to spy on her idiot husband.

"Right. She was a client. So what's your ask?"

Chila shifted closer to his desk. "I have a payout for a policy beneficiary. A man named Woodrow Hassan. I can't seem to track him down. It's like he just ceased to exist."

"I'm not really a research guy," Slater said.

"This isn't a typical research job. I used the company's resources to dig as far as I could in public databases. There are records of him, here and in New Hampshire, and then he just disappears. But he didn't die—at least not that any official record shows."

"If it's an insurance payout, why do you need me to work privately?"

"I was told to let it go, not to waste company time on it." Her eyes grew wide, and she held his gaze. "That means Mr. Hassan will never get his money. It just doesn't seem fair."

People acted like this when they were trying to look guileless, Slater thought, watching her talk. It usually meant they weren't.

"So can you help me?" Chila said, her gaze unwavering.

He pursed his lips for a moment. "Can you give me a grand to get started?"

"I can send it to your phone number."

"I'd rather have cash."

"I don't walk around with that kind of money," Chila said, her brow furrowing, "especially in this neighborhood, when it's almost dark out."

"This isn't really Skid Row. Technically it's the Fashion District. Every other business in this building is a sewing factory."

"Well, it's full of shifty-looking Latin guys."

"They're working people, not thieves," Slater said. His eyes narrowed. "I thought you were Latin."

"My people are Mexican, but not *that* kind of Mexican."

He stifled a retort, something about how eye-opening it was that racism could be so multilayered and nuanced. Even though it was painful to figuratively bite his tongue, things usually went more smoothly when he forced himself to go through the motions of civility. Rolling open his top desk drawer, he grabbed a business card and slid it across to her.

"That number will work."

Eyeing the card, Chila tapped at her phone.

"Send me the guy's name," he said, "and anything else you know about him."

"It's for the greater good, Slater, and I can't do it on my own. I really appreciate your help." She looked up at him, eyes wide, and blinked slowly.

"You're pretty good," he said. The doe eyes probably worked with some people, especially straight guys, but to him it made it feel like this was a snow job.

"What do you mean?"

He waved a hand. "You're convincing."

Sitting back, she furrowed her brow. "I don't need to be convincing. I just gave you a thousand dollars."

"Which means I'll get started. It might be a couple days, though. I'm in the middle of a torrid romance."

"Nice," Chila said. "Who's the lucky gal?"

Slater frowned. "I'm on dick, sister."

"What does that mean?"

"I only fuck guys."

Chila rose. "Well, I'll leave you to it. I wouldn't want you to waste such flowery romantic language on me."

He followed her into the front office, and once she was gone, flipped the bolt on the door. Back at his desk he typed up some notes about her—what she'd said about her target, and the hard sell, and the reference to Marisol. Thinking about it, that alone could be a huge red flag. Marisol had tried to manipulate him into croaking her husband. An endorsement from her was suspicious by definition.

His phone had buzzed a while ago, and he looked at it now. It was a notification about the money Chila had sent. At the bottom of his case notes, he added the date, along with "gave you a deposit, $1 G."

He needed to roll, he realized, checking the time. On the way out he glanced into the other office, where his business partner, Max, worked. The desk was the same as his, but the paint job, in warm yellow, was more appealing than his own, done in turquoise. Maybe it just felt that way because the grass was always greener. Max's office also had the only window, but he didn't care about that. Stepping into the hall, he flipped the lights off, and as he twisted his key to bolt the door, he admired their names emblazoned on it:

SLATER IBÁÑEZ

MAXIMILLIAN CONROY

INVESTIGATIONS

Once he'd ridden the elevator down, he strode through the building's lobby, empty at this hour, and crossed the street to the surface lot where he parked his wheels—a sleek black Thunderbird. Slater loved how it looked, the classic lines and the cherry interior, even though it was far from subtle, and in his business a high-visibility ride could be a liability. He started the throaty engine and flicked on the headlights, then pulled into the street.

The traffic was moving at this time of night, well after business hours, and when he got to the freeway he gunned it and merged left, heading west. Eventually he was in the congested snarl of roadways at LAX, and leaned over the steering wheel, peering out at the new arrivals clotting the sidewalk as he crept along the curb. A double line of cars, trunks and doors open, loading and unloading bodies and luggage, sat between him and the crowd.

Up ahead he spotted Pike when he raised his hand in the air. He punched the gas and roared ahead a few yards, then pulled in.

Pike was wearing a white dress shirt, a few buttons open at the collar, and dark chinos. Maybe he'd left straight from his office. With short dark hair, he had the beefy paunch of a desk jockey. The sight of that easy smile made his heart pound.

Climbing out, Slater embraced him, and rubbed his fists on his back as Pike squeezed him, then met his mouth. It hadn't been that long since they'd been together, but he couldn't get enough of this, and felt his dick tightening in his jeans.

"Let's keep it moving," a man's voice shouted.

Pike pulled away, flushed and grinning, and nodded to the traffic cop, standing on the pavement and waving his arms, tasked with marshaling the chaotic interface between the sidewalk and the vehicles. Pike opened the Thunderbird's passenger door, and pulled the seat ahead, and lifted his bag into the backseat.

Once they'd both climbed in, Slater nosed into the traffic.

"You can see this old flivver coming a mile away," Pike said. "Cars don't have round headlights anymore."

"The term is *classic*," Slater said. "Not old."

"It feels good to be here." Pike reached over and squeezed his shoulder. "You're not going to make me help you decorate some more, are you?"

"You can't deny that I needed window treatments," Slater said. "Otherwise your junk would be on display for the whole neighborhood. Without drapes you need sunglasses indoors, so you'd have to get up with the sun too. I had no idea owning a house was so damn much work."

Exiting the freeway just north of downtown Los Angeles, Slater navigated onto a winding street that climbed the hill from Sunset. Technically his new neighborhood was Echo Park, but he couldn't see the lake from his place, although the deck upstairs had a view of the hills.

The street had some mid-century apartment buildings and some new construction, but the staid Victorians spilling over from Angelino Heights showed the age of the neighborhood, along with the sprawling old Indian laurels. He'd seen a magnolia up the block, and jacarandas at the corner. It was going to be colorful here next spring.

Nosing into his garage, Slater climbed out and hit the button to roll the door down. Pike pulled his bag out of the back, and they climbed the stairs to the second floor, where there were two bedrooms. Stepping into the one Slater used, Pike set down his bag. Slater had picked it because this one had a window over the street, even though the back bedroom was quieter.

"Come upstairs," Slater said, and Pike followed him up.

The house's top floor was mostly one big space, with kitchen counters and appliances near the top of the stairs, then a dining table and chairs, and beyond them an expanse of open floor stretching to a trio of French doors onto the rooftop deck. At one side was a sofa, a couple of lounge chairs, and a TV set, but otherwise he'd left the space open.

Around the sides of the big room Slater had placed cut flowers, a dozen big bunches standing in glass vases.

"Look at all this," Pike said, taking it in. "It smells like a garden in here. It must have cost a fortune."

"The wholesale flower district is right near my office," Slater said. "Most of these were getting old. I got a discount."

"A volume discount too, I'm thinking. Are those irises?"

"It's late in the year for those. Maybe that's why they were cheap."

"You did this for me?" Pike said, meeting his gaze.

"For us."

Stepping closer and grasping his waist, Pike embraced him, and nuzzled his neck.

"You're intense, Ibáñez," he murmured.

Slater tilted his head, and sighed with pleasure, relishing the sensation of his mouth, the warmth of his skin.

"Is it too much?"

Pike pulled back and met his eye. "I can handle it. I can handle you."

Sliding a hand into his hair, Slater kissed him, then grasped his shoulders. "Do you want to eat something? You've been in the air for a while."

"I want you."

"Rosa changed the sheets today."

"I want you right here," Pike said, "in this room, with all the foliage."

Slater wanted to go grab a blanket, but Pike was already unbuttoning his shirt, and kicked off his shoes, and ditched his trousers. Slater sat on the wood floor to untie his boots. Naked now except for his open billowing dress shirt, Pike straddled him, and unbuckled Slater's belt, and popped open his fly, moving with the urgency of not having seen him for a while.

Pike was already hard, and Slater grasped his cock as he leaned down to meet his mouth. Pulling away, Pike ground his wood into Slater's belly, then sat back to yank his jeans off.

Stretching out beside him, Pike locked their mouths together, and Slater wrapped an arm around his neck, and took hold of his cock. Pike grabbed his and then squeezed them together, stroking them both, increasing the speed and the intensity until he yelped and came. Slater soon followed, and grabbed Pike's hand to get him to stop.

Rolling onto his back, he felt his muscles starting to relax, sinking into the cool floor.

"I've been thinking about that all week," Pike said, still breathing hard.

"Tell me about it."

"It happened fast." He pushed his arm under Slater's neck. "We're like a couple of damn teenagers."

He closed his eyes, and his breathing started to

slow. This was the best feeling, the warm moment of satiety.

"Do you want a towel?" Pike said eventually, running a hand over his belly.

"I'm OK for a minute."

The bare floor wasn't actually that uncomfortable. The wood felt cool after a summer day.

Pike didn't move, and Slater reached for his hand, interlacing their fingers. The ceiling was flat gyprock, the same as the walls, he realized, gazing up at it. His old place had that asbestos popcorn stuff. He hadn't even noticed this when he'd first looked the place over.

He'd bought this house when he'd decided to get into things with Pike. He needed space for the relationship, room for Pike, room for things to happen. His dank old one-bedroom only had room for him. It was like hard-packed neglected earth where nothing grew. This place was fresh, and loose, and fertile. Plus he'd had the cash lying around to make the down payment. The only problem was going to be farther down the road, when Pike dumped him—this house might feel too much like them together, and he'd have to move again.

TWO

SLATER WOKE TO DAYLIGHT streaming in his bedroom window. Even with the drapes it got bright in here. Only the thin inner ones were closed, he saw, with the heavier ones pushed open. Sheers, Pike had called them. Why anybody needed two sets of drapes was beyond him; the sheers hardly blocked the light at all.

Lying there, he enjoyed the comfort of the bed, gradually waking up. His head didn't hurt, even though he remembered taking a couple of pulls on the bourbon bottle before he'd crashed. He must not have drunk that much, trying to stick to his booze rules, and behaving himself for Pike. Where was Pike?

Pushing himself off the bed, he pulled on a pair of underpants and a T-shirt, then climbed the stairs to the kitchen. Pike was in his skivvies too, bare-chested, doing something at the range.

"

"You went shopping," he said, glancing at Slater as he stepped in.

"I asked Rosa to do it. I told her I had a house guest."

"Breakfast is going to be hash browns and toast and OJ. I fried a tomato too. Is that weird?"

Stepping up behind him, Slater wrapped his arms around him, caressing his chest and his belly. Pike leaned back into him for a moment. His skin was warm, and Slater breathed in the heady scent of his hair.

He released his grip and went over to the coffeemaker. Pike had already brewed a pot, so he grabbed a mug and poured java from the carafe. This was another concession to civility, although Pike was the one who'd actually bought the machine. He had to admit that it made decent coffee compared to the powdered version he used to drink.

After they'd eaten, sitting adjacent at the dining table next to the kitchen, Slater pushed his plate away.

"I need to do some work today."

Pike gestured with his half-eaten crust. "Go for it."

"I don't want to. I want to stay with you."

"I'm working too. I'm going to catch up on reports, and I have to make some calls. People in Albuquerque are already at their desks." He took the last bite of his toast. "We can't let what we're doing interfere with your job. You'll start to resent me."

Slater slid off his chair, and knelt in front of

him, pushing between his knees, and wrapped his arms around Pike's waist. He kissed his sweaty belly and held him tightly for a moment.

"That's not going to happen."

Once he'd dressed, in jeans and a dark dress shirt, Slater trotted down the stairs to the garage and backed the Thunderbird into the street. The drive downtown took just a little longer than it used to from Westlake, and he took Sunset most of the way, cruising into the Financial District and down into the garage under the tower where Cudahy Mutual had its offices.

He rode up to the thirty-fourth floor and found Della's receptionist, Crystal, on the front desk, looking polished and icy in a dark blue suit, her blond hair swept up in a beehive.

As Slater walked out of the elevator lobby, she looked up and frowned in recognition.

"If you're looking for the soup kitchen," Crystal said, "It's down the block."

Slater paused in front of her desk. "You should do stand-up. And it'll be a frosty day in hell before I take dining advice from you. Is she in?"

The receiver already in hand, Crystal spoke into it. "One of your freelance thugs is here. Shall I call security?"

Hanging up, she flashed him a wan smile. "Go on back."

He scoffed and strode into the hallway, then rapped on Della's half-open office door. She sat back in her chair as he stepped in. Around sixty, maybe, her hair was styled back, and today she was wearing a low-cut summery print blouse.

"You look good," Della said, beaming at him. "Are you here to sniff around for work?"

As he dropped into the chair across from her, he took in the dramatic view from her window, the basin stretching away to the horizon, concrete and asphalt and flecks of greenery baking in the summer sun.

"I'll take it if you've got it, but I'm here on another matter. A client told me she works in the insurance industry. I wondered if you had a back channel to check on whether that's true."

"I can probably find out. What's the name?"

"Isidra Suárez," Slater said. "She goes by Chila."

Della sat up and pulled a coil-bound steno pad out of a drawer, and scrawled down the details, asking him to spell Chila's name.

"Her business card says her company is called Westside Title Guarantee."

"I don't know that one. Let me make some calls."

"Should I wait?"

"No," she said intently, and looked up at him. "I'm juggling a dozen hot potatoes. I can't prioritize this."

"I guess I shouldn't really complain," Slater said, "seeing as you're the boss."

"That strikes me as a calm reaction from you. I thought you might try to strongarm me." She raised an eyebrow. "Not that I'd complain."

"You know me better than that." Slater sat up. "I might actually be a little calmer than usual. I think I'm in love."

"Oh, that is so sweet," she said, her voice rising. "Can I meet him?"

"Not yet. It's pretty new."

"So what's he like?"

"I don't know. He's kind of …" Slater gestured helplessly. "Everything. I can't really be objective. I can't get him out of my head. I bought drapes, and a coffeemaker."

Della chuckled. "You've got it bad. I'm glad it's reciprocal. If it doesn't work out, you should head straight over here. I'm quite skilled at rebound affairs."

"I'll keep that in mind," Slater said, and stood up. "But don't hold your breath."

She pointedly looked him up and down. "I guess it would have to be a pretty gnarly train wreck to make you turn straight. But oh, what I could do to your body."

"Hey," he snapped, in mock indignation, and pointed at his face. "My eyes are up here."

She laughed and scooted her chair closer to her desk. "Later, Slater."

Downstairs in the garage, he climbed into his car and checked the navigation app. It sent him a different way almost every time, presumably routing him around traffic. Today it told him to stay off the freeway, so he took Fig to Sunset. Pulling up at his house, he waited for the door to roll up, then nosed into the garage.

Once he'd hustled up the stairs, he found Pike out on the deck, dressed now, in a gray polo shirt and drab green cargo shorts. He definitely needed to take this guy clothes shopping. Sitting up in a sun lounger with his laptop, Pike's phone was on the ground next to him. He'd shifted the lounger to get the best view, out over the hilly neighborhood, and in the distance, through the haze, the towers of downtown.

"It's not too warm out here?" Slater said as he stepped outside.

"I'm a desert rat, so it feels reasonable to me," Pike said. "I love the sound of the wind in the palms. I keep thinking I'm on a tropical beach."

"Those must be in people's yards. Palms aren't really street trees in this neighborhood."

Slater straddled the lounger, and sat facing him, and leaned in, ravishing him. Pike sighed as Slater mouthed his jaw, and his ear, and his neck.

The soft chime of a bell sounded, and Slater pulled back.

"Was that your phone?"

"It was inside. It sounded like your doorbell."

"I didn't know I had one. I guess it makes sense there would be." He stood up. "That'll be the workers. I'm having the garage door replaced."

"What's wrong with the one that's there now?"

"Not secure enough," Slater called back, and stepped in through the French doors.

When he hustled down the stairs and out the front door, he found a white work truck parked in front of his garage. It had toolbox compartments, and a ladder strapped along the top, and a steel shutter rolled up in the back. Two pasty white guys were climbing out, and he stepped over to greet them.

Most of the manual labor in this town was done by Latin Americans, but Svetlana used her own people, and these two were clearly Russians. From her workshop in a seedy part of Glendale, she was his main supplier of illicit tech—audio bugs, discreet cameras, vehicle trackers, and the software to back it all up. She'd cut him a deal on the garage door too, likely because she knew he kept an array of her stuff in here, and that gear being secure protected her too.

A black Navigator with tinted windows rolled up behind the truck. The rear door opened and Svetlana stepped out. Curvy, with her hair tied back, she was wearing a red-and-yellow print dress, and black wrap-around sunglasses, a bulky black handbag over one arm.

"You're here in the flesh," Slater said, stepping over. "I don't think I've ever seen you outside your workshop."

"I'm not going to do the labor myself," she said, in her lilting Slavic accent, "but I wanted to see your new residence."

"I'll give you the tour."

"My boys can get started if you open the garage door."

Slater went in the front entrance and stepped into the garage, where he hit the button to roll up the big door.

"Can they move your car?" Svetlana said, standing with the workers.

He pulled out his keys and tossed them to the closest guy, who snagged them out of the air.

Svetlana spoke to them in Russian, and both of them nodded assent.

"We'll put the gas traps at the top," she said to Slater, gesturing to the door frame. "Same ones that were in your apartment."

"Excellent," he said. "Come on up."

The other worker had a cordless drill in hand, and as Slater led Svetlana up the stairs, he could hear them starting to disassemble the hardware of the existing door.

"This house looks like a children's building block," Svetlana said, trudging up behind him. "And so many stairs."

He showed her the bedrooms, then led the way up to the kitchen.

"Lots of open space," she said, looking around. "And many flowers. I didn't know you were so sentimental."

"I got them on discount."

She stepped over to the French doors. "Such a lovely view, and bright light. It's like an eagle's nest. I think you must be making money. My rates will have to increase."

"Let's not do that," Slater said. "Most of my money is going to the bankers now."

Folding his laptop closed, Pike got up, and stepped inside, greeting her with a smile. So upbeat, this guy, Slater thought. Always ready with that smile. He didn't understand it, how someone could have that baked in, that degree of positivity, especially in a job where people shot at you. In most people it would just be an annoyance, but in Pike it was compelling, and made him more attractive.

Svetlana introduced herself, then looked him over. *"Menty,"* she said. "You are law enforcement. Maybe a federal agent, I think."

Pike raised his eyebrows. "And you must be psychic."

"It's your style." She waved a hand at his torso, then shot Slater a questioning look.

"He's not here to interrogate me or anything," Slater said. "He's a friend."

"A romantic friend, I'm thinking. This explains the flowers." She gestured to the room, then eyed Slater. "We have an expression in the old country: unless you get caught stealing, you're not a thief."

"Who's the thief in this scenario?" Pike said.

Slater waved a hand. "You mean cops and robbers don't mix."

"I'm saying don't get caught. My boys will give you the radio device to open the garage door when they're finished." She made a little bow to Pike. "A pleasure to meet you, officer."

Slater followed her down to the street. The Thunderbird was at the curb now in front of the next house. The guys had already completely removed the door and were in the process of bolting up the heavier framework for the steel version they'd brought.

Svetlana briefly spoke to them, then stepped toward the Navigator. Walking over with her, Slater pulled open the door for her.

"Is your Mr. Pike one of the clean ones?" she said as she climbed in.

"I think so."

"Then you might have a security problem."

"I keep him separate from that part of my life," Slater said. "He doesn't know much about my work, and he'll never see any of your equipment."

"I'm glad you're thinking this way," she said, and pulled the door closed.

He watched the Navigator pull away. Did she have a driver because she didn't know how to drive herself, or was it just because she could afford to? When he walked back up the stairs, Pike was in the kitchen, standing at the counter.

"Do you want a fake cheese sandwich?" he said, gesturing with a knife. "Rosa bought sourdough."

Slater frowned. "Just because there's no animal products in it doesn't mean it's fake."

"Got it. Do you want 'mayonnaise'?" he said, waggling his fingers to put air quotes around the word.

Folding his arms, Slater scoffed.

Pike glanced back at him, his brow furrowing. "What's with you?"

"I wish you hadn't met her. She made you as a G-man in a hot second. It might screw up my business."

"In my world, that implies she's up to some-thing."

"She helps me with security. Nothing more." Slater waved an arm. "Svetlana once said, 'Not my circus, not my monkeys.'"

His eyes narrowed. "You're saying she's none of my business."

"Just forget about her. Forget you even met her."
Pike turned and handed him a plate with a sandwich on it. "Met who?"

THREE

A WHILE AFTER THEY'D EATEN, a voice called up the stairs: "Hey, boss."

When Slater went down to the street, he found that they'd moved his car back inside. One of the guys demonstrated the door rolling up and down, pressing the wall switch. It definitely looked more secure than the basic hardware store version they'd taken down.

The guy pointed out the tear-gas traps at the top, one on either side. The gray plastic blended in with the metal components, and subtle green LEDs showed they were armed.

"It looks great," Slater said. "The motor is really quiet."

"Call Sveta if you have any problems." He handed over the garage-door opener and his car keys.

As they climbed into the truck, Slater hit the

button to roll the door down, then heard Pike descending the stairs. Stepping into the garage, he came over and rapped on the new door with a knuckle.

"That's heavy duty."

"When the junkies come looking for copper to steal, they're not going to get inside."

"Not unless they have a battle bus." Pike stepped back, looking over the steel shutter and the lift components, and pointed up at one of the tear-gas traps. "What's that?"

"Of course you'd notice that, you big snoop. Anything that didn't come from the hardware store."

He raised his eyebrows. "So what is it?"

"It's a sensor that'll tell me if the door opens when I'm not around."

Pike stepped closer and craned his neck. "I can see the sensor. There's also a compressed gas cylinder attached." He eyed Slater. "You know this is in my wheelhouse, right? Stuff that blows up?"

Slater huffed. "They're tear-gas traps. If someone breaks in, they'll get doused with tear gas. It's meant to slow down the burglars."

His eyes narrowed. "I'm pretty sure that's illegal."

"Like Sveta said, only if I get caught."

"I was thinking about what she said. If I'm the cop, that means she thinks you're the robber."

"I don't steal, son," Slater said flatly.

Pike looked up at them again. "I guess it's not really any of my business."

"That's such a good attitude."

"Who came up with this?"

"It's a standard security item," Slater said.

"No, it's not," he said firmly, and met his gaze.

"Listen, you need to let it go. I have more stuff to do out in the world."

"All right." Pike laughed. "I'm working today too."

"What's funny?" Slater demanded.

"You. Us. I'm really enjoying all this getting to know you. Your garage is more secure than most bank vaults."

Slater stepped closer, and squeezed his biceps. "I'm really enjoying getting to know your dick."

Pike laughed again, his tone deep and rich. "Me too. But it's more than that."

"Much more," Slater said softly, leaning in until their foreheads were touching, feeling his warm breath on his face. "No terminal red flags yet?"

"Ain't nothing stopping this freight train." Pike ran his fingers into his hair. "I can't keep my hands off you."

Pulling away, Slater swatted his butt. "If you need to eat something more substantial, there's lots of places to get food on Sunset."

"I'm actually a grown man, and I have cash. I can figure out how to get fed."

Slater pursed his lips. "That actually has the ring of truth."

He chuckled. "I managed to do it for years before I met you."

As Pike stepped into the stairwell, he climbed into the Thunderbird, and started the engine, and waited for the new door to roll up. Once he had the air-conditioning cranked, he drove downtown again, and parked in the surface lot behind Andy's building, and walked around to the entrance on Broadway.

Upstairs, he knocked on Andy's door, and waited until he pulled it open. Wearing a tank top and boxer shorts, Andy was lithe, with stubble on his face, his brown hair a perpetual perfect mess.

Slater followed him inside, watching his uneven gait and admiring his butt. The place had big multipane windows and wooden floors from its first incarnation as a textile warehouse. The loft conversion made this unit mostly one open space, with the far corner dominated by a computer desk and monitors.

Andy sat in his gaming chair. He didn't actually play video games, he said, but its ergonomics helped him with his posture during his long hours at the computer.

"Is your boyfriend in town?" Andy said, his brow furrowing.

Slater stood in front of him, hands on his hips. "He's not my boyfriend."

"That's not how you … explained it to me."

"So maybe he is." He waved a hand. "I don't know yet."

Andy jabbed a finger at him. "You are an emotional wreck."

"I know," he said softly, and looked away.

"Well, it pisses me off."

Slater took a breath. He didn't know what to say. He could feel his heart pounding.

"It's like I'm not enough," Andy said, and threw up a hand. "And you … picked someone else."

"I can't explain it. I think the guy has some kind of pheromone imbalance. I can't keep my hands off him."

"You should have picked me."

"It's not like I'm exclusive with him. We can still mess around."

"Have you cleared … that with him?"

Kneeling in front of him, Slater reached for his thighs, and started to massage them. Andy punched him hard, in the shoulder. He had good aim considering his lack of fine motor control. Slater sat back on his heels and scowled at him.

"Ow."

"You're an asshole," Andy shouted.

"I know." Slater took a breath. "I'm not even sure if it's going to work out. I don't have a great track record with men."

"So you want to keep … all your options open, just in case."

"I don't want to stop seeing you just because there's someone else."

"Plus you need me to … work for you."

He swallowed the lump in his throat, unable to dislodge it. "The last thing I wanted to do was hurt you."

"It's too … late. No love without pain, remember?"

"What about that trash-bag gunsel Kyle? You've been fucking him most of the time I've known you."

"He's not you," Andy said, and leaned forward, and jabbed his shoulder again with a sharp knuckle.

"But he wants you. I know he wants you all to himself. That's why he hates me, and calls me a booze hag. He thinks I'm a bad influence on you."

"I want to meet this ... out-of-town interloper."

"His name is Pike."

"I don't fucking care," Andy said, raising his voice. "You should bring him ... over here. Maybe if I could meet him I wouldn't be ... so pissed."

"Like a hookup, or just a meet-and-greet?"

"Is he hot?"

Slater sighed. "In some cultures I suppose he might be considered interesting."

"So he's a smoke show. Of course ... he is." Andy scoffed. "I fucking knew it."

"I'm not sure he'll be up for a three-way. I'll ask."

"Why are you here?" he demanded.

"Work."

"I've got ... other clients. Other stuff to do."

"Like what?"

"Contract work for an ... oil company."

Slater groaned. "Watch your back. Whenever I've had to deal with that industry, there's lots of goons."

"I'm not really out in the field like ... you are."

"Still, if you dig too deep, or piss off the wrong suit, you wind up in an oil drum at the bottom of the bay."

"I'm not doing that kind of work."

Slater stood up. "So do you have time for my stuff or not?"

"What's the task?"

He explained Chila's story about Woodrow Hassan, and that she couldn't find any trace of him, and that there was no death record.

"When was the last time he had an ID?"

"That wasn't one of the details she gave me. Do you think you could do a deep dive?"

"All you have is the guy's name?"

"My client said she tracked him to Manchester, New Hampshire, and then he just disappears."

"I'll see what I can … find out."

"Soon, or next month? I don't need your passive-aggressive bullshit. If you can't do it, say so right now."

"I said I'd … look into it." Andy frowned. "I have some time today."

"Just make it so that I don't have to go there."

"New Hampshire? Why not? The Northeast is beautiful in summer. Lush and leafy and green."

"If you like humidity," Slater said, "and mosquitoes, and yellow fever."

"They might have sorted out the … yellow fever thing sometime after … George Washington left office."

"If you say so." Slater hesitated—he wanted to kiss him before he left, taste those beautiful lips. But Andy was too upset. Instead he waved a hand and walked out.

WHEN SLATER GOT BACK to his place, he saw Max's matte-gray Challenger parked at the curb, just past the driveway.

"Idiot," he muttered. Max should have called him if he needed to see him. He got enough face time with the guy at the office.

After the garage door had rolled down, he hustled up the stairs, and into the kitchen. Through the French doors he could see Pike with Max and Etta, sitting around the patio table. Etta was curvy and had her dark hair butched short, and today, out in the sunshine, she was wearing a pair of aviator sunglasses. Slater had brought her on as a part-time operative, and she had good sense for the work, and had the requisite level of sangfroid. Her people were Samoan, so she understood how small communities operated, and her full-time gig was as an educator, so she knew how to bring out the best in people, how to motivate them without using her fists the way Slater did. These days she worked more with Max, on his window-shade jobs, stalking cheaters for jealous spouses.

Max was thick, and sweaty, with mousy brown hair, his sidearm bulging under his jacket. There was no mistaking his job: Max was the heavy. At least he was wearing his light seersucker suit today in the heat.

Approaching the French doors, he saw there were glasses on the table, and a big bottle of lemonade. It was infuriating that he had no idea what had been said here so far.

As he stepped out, Slater said, "What's going on?"

"We came to see your new pad," Etta said.

"I'm not sure why you need to see the place. I've never been in your apartment."

"You never bought a house before," Max said. "It's kind of a big deal."

"Have some lemonade," Pike said, a wry smile on his face, and waved him to the fourth chair.

There was a glass for him, Slater saw, and he poured into it from the bottle.

"This place is beautiful," Etta said, "but it's completely obnoxious. It's a monolith to gentrification."

"I'm sure the neighbors resent it too," Slater said, and gestured with his glass. "Some idiot hipsters built it and then ran out of money. I think I got a deal because the bank wanted to unload it."

"You didn't build it, so you're not the gentrifier," Max said. "If you hadn't bought it someone else would have."

"Still, Etta's right. I'm benefiting from the dis-placement of whoever lived here before." He sighed. "I know it's a shrine to civilian life. It's as far out of the cesspool as I could reach."

"Just because you work in the cesspool doesn't mean you need to live in it," Max said.

Etta sat up, folding her arms on the table. "When I got here, I went to the door on the other side of your garage, and an old woman answered. I thought she was burgling you. Then I realized it has a different house number."

"It's a separate unit," Slater said. "A ground-floor one-bedroom. Kind of next to the garage and behind it."

"So you have a tenant."

"That's Grace, my neighbor in Westlake."

"You brought her with you?" Etta said, her brow furrowing.

"I went to say good-bye, and we got talking. I was shocked at how much rent she was paying. I couldn't just leave her there."

"Plus you're a control freak," Etta said. "But that is sweet of you. I didn't think you did actual human relationships."

Slater frowned. "I don't. Not that kind. It's transactional. My thinking is that Grace has twenty years on Doris. When that sweet chariot swings low for Grace, Doris might be ready to downsize, and the apartment will open up."

"You must have more of a connection to her than that," Pike said.

"Grace was actually in the life," Max said. "She spent time in Vegas. Slater uses her as an operative sometimes."

"It's an excellent cover," Slater said. "The doddering old woman. She's sharp, and agile, but she can really play it up."

"I met her for a hot minute," Pike said. "She seemed pleasant. It's hard to imagine her as a con artist."

Slater waved a hand. "That makes her better at it. She once faked a heart attack as a distraction for me, and gave me fifteen solid minutes when no one paid attention to anything but her."

"That sounds like some serious acting chops," Pike said.

Etta slapped the table. "Let's ask her to come up."

"Oh, hell no," Slater said. "It's not that kind of relationship."

"But you've made it that kind of relationship," she said. "What if you go broke and this place gets foreclosed, or god forbid, you get iced? She'll have to move again. You've put her at your mercy."

"Grace doesn't have to worry about money," Max said.

"What does that mean?"

Max eyed Slater. "Tell her."

"It feels like gossip," Slater said, and shifted in his chair. "Some guy in Vegas—"

"It has to be a gangster," Max said.

"Some probably a gangster in Vegas, maybe a boyfriend, maybe she married him, I don't know the details, anyway, he set up a trust fund for her. She's got some dough."

"They split up?" Pike said.

Slater waved a hand. "He's in the fertilizer business."

"Like gardening?" Etta said. "Do gangsters run businesses like that?"

"Everybody does eventually," Max said. "He means he's dead."

Etta nodded. "Was she a showgirl?"

"I think she kept the books," Slater said. "Both sets."

"So she'd know exactly where the skeletons were," Max said.

"Is she paying you rent?" Etta said.

"None of your damn business, but yes, she's chipping in."

Pike sat up. "Do you want to have a celebratory drink with your colleagues? You can't toast with lemonade."

"Great idea," Slater said, and stood up. "I'll get it."

Etta followed him inside, leaving the French doors ajar, and pushed her sunglasses up into her hair.

"What's with all the flowers?" she said as they walked to the kitchen.

"I was driving by the flower market. It was late in the day. They were getting rid of them. I basically saved all these from the Dumpster."

"I can't believe you fit all this in your car."

"I had them delivered."

She waved her arm at the room. "Why?"

"What's wrong with flowers?" Slater demanded. "I thought it was fitting for a torrid love affair."

Etta chuckled. "You're a romantic. I've never seen that in you before."

"I'm not sure what's going on," he said, pulling tumblers out of the kitchen cabinet. "I feel like I'm high all the time, and my heart is messed up." He handed her the stack of glasses. "Like, physically. Like it's beating too much."

"It's called love, Slater."

He scoffed. "Whatever the hell that means."

In the pantry cupboard he grabbed the bottle of good scotch and followed Etta back outside. He poured for the four of them, and they tapped glasses.

"Congrats on all this," Max said.

This was good stuff, Slater realized, sipping at the satisfying nutty elixir. Another contribution from Pike, something that Slater would never invest in. It was too pricey to justify drinking instead of his quotidian cheap-ass applejack, considering how much of it he drank.

Etta set down her tumbler and waggled a finger at him and Pike. "So how did you two meet, exactly?"

"We met at a dinner party held by some friends of mine," Slater said. "At first Pike thought I was this snob from Newport."

Max frowned. "Friends? Dinner parties?" He threw up a hand. "Who are you?"

Pike laughed. "That's what Jackie said about

how she met JFK. We watched a documentary about her last night."

"Since when do you watch TV?" Etta demanded. "In your pad in Westlake you said you didn't even have a TV."

"You can't just have sex all the time, Etta," Slater said. "You need to take breaks."

"Well, that's new too," Max said.

Slater shot him a look.

"We met on my case," Pike said. "I was tracking down a domestic terrorist named Galliform."

"We actually met on my case," Slater said. "I was tracking Galliform. The feds stumbled into it and pulled rank."

They talked some more, and finished the round of scotch. It was interesting to see Max and Etta out of work mode. They felt lighter, and laughed more. Maybe his perception was distorted by whatever was happening with Pike, he realized. The rose-colored glasses. Watching Pike, his animated conversation, his deep laugh, he saw that the guy was good at this, good at connecting with people. The parade of shrinks Doris had sent him to in his youth would likely tell him that it was important, this part—socializing, Pike getting to know his crew, building familiarity.

———◆———

By the time Max and Etta left, twilight was setting in. Slater locked the front door behind them, and climbed the stairs behind Pike.

"I'm so not used to that."

"Day drinking?" Pike said.

"That, I'm completely comfortable with. I'm not used to all the chitchat. We work together, and usually we talk business."

"Networking is part of the deal." Pike stopped on the landing where the bedrooms were. "Drinking with them builds trust, and makes your work relationship more solid."

"Did they teach you that at the academy?"

Pike shrugged. "It's just common sense."

"You're such a cop."

Stepping closer, Pike put his hands on Slater's waist. "And you love it."

"I kind of do. Do you want to detain me?"

Pike mouthed his neck, and fumbled with Slater's belt, unbuckling it. "I don't have my cuffs."

"I've got lots."

Pulling away, Slater walked into his bedroom and pulled open a drawer in the bedside table. He dug around to find a pair, then tossed them to Pike.

"Nice," he said, looking them over. "They're not like cop ones."

"They're a lot more comfortable."

Slater ditched his jeans and pulled off his shirt and tossed it on the floor. Eyeing Pike, he curled his lip into a sneer, and groped his own cock, and jutted his chin at him, a tacit challenge. Pike stepped over and grabbed his wrist, and deftly twisted him around, seizing his other arm. Slater let him click the cuffs on. He was already getting hard.

Pike pushed him onto the bed, and pulled his own shirt off, and ditched his fuggly cargo shorts.

Slater lay there watching him, on his side, his hands firmly bound in the small of his back. Naked now, Pike stroked his own cock, and held his gaze, his eyes hard. Standing at the edge of the bed, he grabbed the back of Slater's head, and pulled him closer, pressing his cock into his face.

Slater took him into his mouth, and smoked him, and Pike moaned, quickly getting harder. As Pike leaned in, cradling his head in his hands, Slater looked up at him, and made his eyes wide, a mock plea for relief, all the while working him hard. That must have done it for Pike, as he leaned closer, then came, his face contorting with the intensity of it. Once his spasming subsided, Slater pulled away and flopped on his side.

"That was so fucking hot," Pike said, and climbed on the bed next to him, and caressed his chest.

Slater ground his cock into his thigh, and Pike took hold of it, and pumped it, and moved close to mouth his neck. He paused for a moment, and sat up on his elbow, and slapped Slater's face.

"Fuck you," Slater growled through his teeth, his cheek burning.

Pike slapped him again, not holding back, then grabbed his cock and increased the pressure. When Slater came, he strained into Pike, and then pulled away, rolling onto his back.

Once his breathing started to slow, he spoke. "Why do you do this to me?"

Pike turned to him. "Do your wrists hurt? I can unhook you."

"It's not that. Why do you make me feel like this?"

Pike ran a hand across his chest, and Slater closed his eyes, sinking into the warm feeling of his touch.

FIVE

IN THE MORNING, WHEN Slater woke, he was in his bed. It took a second to figure out that his phone was ringing. That's what had summoned him to consciousness. The distinctive ring tone made his heart sink: *No wire hangers! I buy you beautiful dresses, and you treat them like they were some dishrag …*

"Damn it," he muttered, and scrabbled for the phone on the bedside table.

Pike was already awake, propped up on the pillows, his own phone in hand.

"Do not tell me you set that ring tone for your mother," he said, and laughed.

Ignoring him, Slater picked up the call. "What do you need, Doris?"

"When you say that, you make it sound like I'm trying to schnorr off you," she said. "Remember who brought you into this world."

"That doesn't answer my question."

"I want to see your house. You must be settled in by now."

He sighed audibly. "I guess you can come over for dinner. But come early so you can see it in daylight."

"Can I bring a plus-one?"

"If you must. Remember I told you about the guy from Albuquerque? He'll be here too."

The volume of her reaction made Slater wince and pull the phone away from his ear, and he soon ended the call.

Pike chuckled. "She's enthusiastic. I want to meet her too."

"I guess it's inevitable," he said, and set the phone down. "She's absolutely thrilled that you're Jewish, by the way."

"It makes sense. She wants her grandchildren to be raised Jewish."

"Slow down, Seabiscuit." Slater shoved the covers down and climbed on top of him, straddling his pelvis. "I'm barely out of knee pants myself."

Pike massaged his arms. "You'd be a great dad."

"I'd be a terrible dad. I do terrible things. I'm not good for people, Pike. Broken people break people."

"You're not that broken. Plus you're slightly hot, if I squint. Partial hotness makes up for a lot."

"Eat a dick," Slater said flatly.

Pike chuckled. "Gladly." He pushed Slater off, then repositioned himself farther down the bed, and went down on him.

Slater folded his arms behind his head. The guy was so good at this, quickly ascertaining the right rhythm. He closed his eyes, relishing the intensity of it, and a moment later arched his back as he climaxed. Pike shifted up beside him, his face red, grinning at him. Slater grabbed his cock and met his warm mouth, stroking him for a minute until he came.

They lay there for a while, warm and content, until Pike got up and padded over to the bathroom. Slater heard the shower go on. Sitting up on his pillows, he grabbed his phone again. Andy had texted:

This might be the guy: Jacob Spiros.

A second text had the name of a Greek restaurant, along with:

He works at this diner.

Chila hadn't said anything about the guy being Greek, but then she hadn't said much about him at all. The phone buzzed in his hand with an incoming call: Della.

"From what I can tell, Isidra Suárez is legit," Della said when he picked up. "She works in mortgage insurance."

"That's real estate. Does your company do that too?"

"It's a whole different thing. A different set of actuaries, and a very different day-to-day experience than over here."

"Did you talk to anyone who knows her?" Slater said.

"Unfortunately not, but I found her name on a list of employees for Westside Title Guarantee. Her office is in Chino."

"That's what her card said too. Not exactly on the Westside."

"I guess you'd call it an aspirational company name. Like how everything west of La Brea is Beverly Hills–adjacent."

Slater ended the call, and got up, and pulled on his jeans and a clean shirt.

Pike was flushed when he came back from his shower, his hair spiky from being toweled.

Slater squatted to tie his boots. "Will you be all right if I leave for a while?"

"I should be able to survive."

"Don't burn the place down. I just bought it."

"Etta's right. You're a control freak."

"And you're Reddy Kilowatt. The man with a million volts in his pants." Slater rose, and held Pike's warm damp head with both hands long enough to kiss him. "Zap."

He trotted down to the Thunderbird and checked the address of the diner Andy had sent. It was way out in the Valley. At least the morning school traffic was over. You'd think in a sprawling metropolis like this somebody would use school buses, but it seemed that every kid younger than driving age got personally chauffeured to school. It made the hour before classes started traffic chaos.

Navigating to the 101, Slater headed north, into the Valley, and eventually exited onto surface streets. This whole neighborhood was Greek, he knew, anchored by a big old Greek Orthodox church. The diner was set back from the street, past a mostly empty parking lot that fronted the boulevard. That was the best thing about the Valley—there was always parking.

Pulling into a stall a few rows back from the entrance, Slater looked the place over. There were only a few other cars here, but a lit sign in the window said OPEN. When he stepped inside he saw that the vibe was more than just a diner. There were tables and booths but also a bar at one side, with a wall of booze bottles. Nobody was sitting there, unsurprisingly this early in the day, but a couple of the booths were occupied. Near the kitchen was a counter with a cash register, staffed by a tall guy in a blue apron, with freckles and an unkempt Afro. Boredom in his eyes, he looked to be in his twenties.

"I need to talk to Spiros," Slater said, stepping over to him.

"Are you a vendor?"

"What's it to you, toots? Is Spiros here or not?"

He scowled and stepped into the kitchen.

A moment later a guy came out a different doorway, at the end of the bar, and nodded to him.

In his fifties, maybe, his black hair was slicked back, and he wore the same apron as the guy on the till. He had a bit of a paunch, but he was basically fuckable.

"I'm an insurance investigator," Slater said, stepping over and handing him his card.

The guy studied it for a moment, then met his gaze. "You like coffee?"

"Are you offering? If you're making Greek coffee, sure, set me up."

"It's interesting that you call it Greek." He set to work below the bar. "Most people say it's Turkish."

"Isn't it Greek?"

He chuckled. "So what kind of insurance issue are you here about?"

"Life insurance. Concerning someone named Woodrow. Have you ever used that name?"

"Do I look like a Woodrow?" He glanced briefly at Slater as he set a pair of little cups on the bar.

"That doesn't answer my question."

"I was born Spiros, and when they plant me in the ground I'll be Spiros. You have the wrong man."

Slater believed him, he decided. The guy showed no spark of recognition, thoroughly unfazed at the mention of Woodrow. "Do you have a son or a father with the same name?"

"There's only one Spiros. It's me."

The scent of hot fresh java was in the air now, and Spiros soon poured from the *briki*, then slid one of the cups across the bar.

"Do you want sugar in it?" Spiros waggled a little spoon.

"Just black."

"Same as me. We call that *sketos*."

"This is really good," Slater said, after he'd taken a sip. "What about New Hampshire?"

He chuckled. "I know it exists. Personally I've never been anywhere near it. Why would you think I used a different name?"

"I think my wires got crossed," Slater said. "Can

I get another one of these to go?"

He nodded and set a paper cup on the bar, then poured again from the *briki*.

"Is someone going to come over here and arrest me for identity theft?" Spiros said.

"Not because of me. I made a mistake. It won't go any farther."

Spiros snapped a plastic lid on the cup, and Slater picked it up, setting a sawbuck on the bar.

"We're having a conversation here." He frowned and gestured broadly. "I would have comped the coffee."

"So put it in the tip jar."

Slater walked to the entrance and stepped outside.

Parked in the stall in front of the Thunderbird was a dark blue moped, and crouching next to it was a scrawny guy with long hair. He stood erect when Slater stepped out, watching him approach. This guy wasn't dressed to ride, and he didn't have a helmet in hand—he was trying to steal it.

That wasn't Slater's problem, and he hadn't even planned to talk to him, but as he got closer, the guy suddenly bolted, running toward the street. Slater ran after him, breaking into a sprint, for no good reason other than instinct. He tried to keep the little paper cup level, holding it away from his body so that it wouldn't spill on him.

Longhair wasn't moving very fast, and Slater saw that his jeans were slowing him down—his belt was hanging halfway down his ass, the crotch of the garment almost to his knees. Why wouldn't he pull his pants up?

Just before he reached the sidewalk, Slater caught up to him, and grabbed his shoulder, and spun him around, shoving him into the chain-link fence, the little cup tumbling to the ground.

The guy yelped and bounced off the fence, and Slater grabbed his biceps, sweeping a boot under him and shoving him to the asphalt. He went down easy. That and the intense wild look in his eye told him the guy was definitely high—tweaking, it looked like, based on his discolored teeth. But he wasn't homeless, as his clothes were reasonably kempt, and he didn't smell.

Slater straddled him, and squatted on his pelvis, holding tight to one of his wrists, then backhanded him, left and then right, a rapid kovac. He slapped at Slater with his free hand, and clawed at his face, but Slater easily seized that wrist too and held firm.

"Why do you make me do this to you?" Slater shouted, and slapped him again.

"I'll put it back," the guy said, screwing his eyes shut and twisting his face away. "Just let me go."

"You made me dump my coffee, you idiot. What's your name?"

"Why does that matter?"

Slater slapped him again. "Are you Spiros?"

"What? Who's Spiros?"

The specific way he was addled looked like it was enhanced by meth, but his bewilderment was genuine, Slater decided. But he'd also implied that he'd stolen something.

"Where did you put it?" Slater demanded.

"Get off me."

He slapped him again. "Sing, brother."

"Stop it," he cried, batting at his hand. "It's at my place."

Groping his pants, Slater found a lump in his front pocket, and dug it out—his wallet. The guy grabbed his wrist but Slater easily wrenched it loose, holding the wallet higher. When he folded it open he found the guy's driver's license.

"Well, Trent, if you don't put it back, I know where you live. Over there on Magnolia." He met his gaze. "You make this right, or I'll come for you."

"I said I would. Now, get off me."

Slater rose, and stepped back, watching as the guy got to his feet. Fuckable, maybe, in a pinch, if he sobered up. He tossed him the wallet. Trent caught it awkwardly, and eyed him for a beat, then trotted out to the sidewalk, finally hiking up his belt, and loped up the block.

Slater couldn't care less what he was up to, or what he'd stolen, but he shouldn't have run. Tweakers were skittish like that.

The lid was still on the little paper cup, he saw, even though it was lying on its side on the asphalt, and he picked it up. It hadn't actually spilled—not a drop. The lid made a tight seal. Andy would be happy.

Carrying it back across the parking lot, he got into the Thunderbird, and started the engine, and nosed it onto the boulevard. Holding his phone in his lap, hopefully low enough to be out of view of any sharp-eyed cop, he dialed Andy's number and put it on speaker.

"So I'm out in the ass end of the Valley," Slater said when he picked up. "The name you gave me was a wrong guy. How old was Spiros supposed to be?"

"You know, I wondered about that," Andy said. "I might have found you … a better lead."

"I'm on my way over."

He ended the call and accelerated up the ramp onto the freeway. Had Andy orchestrated that snipe hunt because he was pissed at him? That would be an ugly freaking trajectory for things to take. Was there some kind of symbolism in sending him to a Greek restaurant? Maybe he just wanted a coffee, and Slater had fallen for it. He couldn't really accuse Andy of doing it intentionally either. That would just make things worse.

SIX

WHEN ANDY OPENED HIS door, Slater held up the paper cup and followed him inside.

"Greek coffee? Sweet. You know what I like."

"Jacob Spiros made it for you." He set the cup on the little table under the windows as Andy sat in his desk chair. "Who the fuck was he? He told me nobody ever called him Woodrow."

"That's a little complicated." Andy waved a hand. "Mistakes … were made."

"By you," he said, raising his voice.

"So I made some tenuous connections, and some … wrong assumptions. It happens. But I found … a much more likely candidate."

"Spill it."

"So you know how New Hampshire is … kind of libertarian," Andy said.

"What does that have to do with my target?"

"If you change your name in Cali, you do it through … the state government. They keep track, so the credit … agencies and the banks and the tax people all know exactly … who you are and who you were. But over there it's some kind of … common-law thing, where your name is whatever you say it is. And the state … may or may not have a record of that."

Slater put his hands on his hips. "So Woodrow changed his name."

"Only his last name. That's how I … found him. There's not a lot of people named Woodrow."

"What's his new name?"

"Woodrow Hassan disappears … after doing a year of college at a state school in Manchester. The next term … a guy named Woodrow Newkirk appears. He's a second year … student, in the same department. Coincidence? I think not."

"So his new name is Newkirk. Are you sure it's the same person?"

"It's him."

"The same way Jacob Spiros was him?"

"Cut me some slack," Andy said. "From the photos it looks … like the same dude."

"Show me." Slater gestured to the computer.

Andy swiveled toward his screens and pulled on his black gauntlets. They were a specialized input device that Andy said made sense of his muscle movements, sifting out the intent from the random noise.

On the screen he pulled up two images. College ID cards, Slater saw, stooping to look closer.

They were from the same college. Each had a portrait photo, and the guy had changed his haircut, but it was definitely the same face. The ID numbers were different, and one bore the name Hassan, the other Newkirk.

"That's totally the same guy," Slater said. "Send me those. How did you get them?"

"You know better than to … ask me that."

"Where is Woodrow now?"

"Right here in la-la land," Andy said. "You won't have to venture into the disease-riddled swamps of the East."

"Lucky for me."

"It's not really surprising. This is his hometown. Woodrow Hassan went to … high school here. In Inglewood. I'm sure there's more work opportunities … here than in smalltown New Hampshire."

"Did you find a current address?"

"I'll text it to you."

"What about where he works, anything like that?"

"Once you know the guy's real name," Andy said, "there's … lots about him online. You can see … that stuff yourself. His home address is in … Hollywood. He's listed as the sole owner."

"I wonder why he changed his name."

Andy shed the gauntlets, and swiveled toward him, and tented his fingers. "That's an excellent question, Slater. I have … a theory. The address he lived at in Inglewood for high school … comes up in court records. The other … residents of that property were … Clive Hassan and Tanisha Hassan."

"His parents?"

"Based on their ages, that fits. Both are … deceased. They died the same year … Woodrow changed his name."

"Why were they named in court proceedings?" Slater said.

"They were both … charged with defrauding a school board."

"Ouch. How was the case resolved?"

"They died before it went … to trial. A single-vehicle wreck in the Angeles National Forest. The car went … straight off a two-hundred-foot cliff. Neither one of them was … wearing a seat belt."

"Murder-suicide, maybe," Slater said, "to avoid the trial and the embarrassment?"

"The police report said it was an accident."

"That just means they found no evidence to show intent."

"I'd probably … change my name too."

Slater nodded. "Good work. Finally."

"You owe me six dollars."

"Damn it," he snapped. "Does that include the I'm-pissed-at-you tax?"

"You saw the kind of data I scraped. For what you're … getting, my rates are more than fair."

Slater dug out his wad of cash. "Can I deduct my mileage for the wild goose chase in the Valley this morning?"

"Pass it on to your … client. You know the drill."

"I want you to look into my client too." He riffled off six C-notes and set them on his desk, then handed him Chila's business card. "Can you copy that?"

Andy swiveled and lifted the top of a scanner, and set the card on the glass, and pressed a button with the heel of his fist.

"Why are you suspicious of her?"

"She hired me to work a life insurance case, but she's in title insurance. That's apples and oranges. She tried to sell me on it with the naive routine. Something about it just doesn't wash."

"What do you want to … know about her?" Andy said, and handed the card back.

"Her title, for one," Slater said, and waggled the card. "This doesn't say what her job is. I've basically got her answer for her now, but before I share it with her, I want to know if she's being straight with me or not."

"I'll work on it today." Andy shifted in his chair. "So do I get to meet … the interloper or not?"

"I can ask him about a three-way. It seems like that would be the least uncomfortable path."

"For you, at least. But I'm … game. Make it tonight."

———•———

ONCE HE WAS DOWN at his car, Slater got the engine running, and the air blowing, then did an online search for Woodrow Newkirk. Like Andy said, there were several results. He quickly ascertained that this guy was in the music business.

One hit was an article that referred to him as Woody, with Woodrow in parentheses. Scrolling down, he found a photo of him, standing with some other people. There was more mileage on him now than in his college days, but it was the same person.

Another article explained that he was a vocalist, and described his voice as "deep, rich, and clear." Woody worked on film scores, it said, and also worked with the house band at Alsace Acres. Slater knew that place well—once a nightclub, now more of a bar and restaurant, it had been there forever.

A notification popped up on his screen—the documentation from Andy about Woody. Swiping through it, he zoomed in on the student ID cards, and then Woody's college transcripts. The guy was no dummy, graded mostly with A's and a couple of B's. It was amazing that Andy could get hold of this stuff. It could be from a data broker, as they compiled anything they could get, but it felt like he'd gone deeper than that.

Woody's home address in Hollywood was in the package, and he plugged it into his navigation app, and pulled out of the parking lot, and headed for the freeway.

It was a little bungalow with a brick-and-iron fenced yard, he found, pulling up on it. He parked across the street, a few houses down, to look the place over. Half of the front yard had been paved for parking, but there was only one vehicle here, a new Bronco. The house looked postwar, maybe eight hundred square feet tops.

Even as a tear-down it was likely worth over a million bucks. This neighborhood was gradually turning, Slater knew, and people with money were renovating and rebuilding. He could see the tops of a couple of boxy modern structures, built as high as the zoning allowed, as close to the property line as legally possible. Just like his own house, he reminded himself. He couldn't very well sneer at gentrification when he was up to his armpits in it too.

The patchy little lawn was dried out and brown. Letting it die was smart—it was so inappropriate here to have water-hungry landscaping. It needed some dryland planting. A day's work would do it. In the middle of the yard was a sprawling olive tree. That was a little unusual, to see one of those in a front yard, but it had been planted long before Woody lived here, long before he'd been born.

No way could a nightclub singer's earnings pay for this house, or any house in this town. And that Bronco was new. It was yellow, not as warm as the mustard walls in Max's office, more like the color they painted construction equipment. Woody definitely had another source of income besides music. But was there any point in talking to this guy? He didn't even know the details of what Chila wanted with him.

The gate across the driveway was open, with the Bronco parked inside. Grabbing his binoculars out of the backseat, he trained them on the license plate, then thumb-typed a note of the number on his phone.

It wasn't safe to put a tracker on the Bronco—there was no cover, and the front curtains of the house were open. He'd seen several pedestrians go by on this street already. Inevitably a neighbor or some passerby would see him do it.

Pulling into the street, he headed back to the freeway, relieved that the traffic was still moving. Exiting into the Fashion District, he drove to his office, and parked in the surface lot across the street from the old high-rise, waving to the attendant as he climbed out. They knew his car, and knew he bought a monthly pass, so he rarely had to interact with them.

A few day laborers were hanging around the building's lobby, waiting for gigs in the clothing factories upstairs. He and Max had the only office that wasn't about the garment industry, and they liked it that way—it was easy to stay out of sight.

Stepping into his office, he flicked on the lights, and double-clicked his tongue to greet the little statue of Rey Pascual on Etta's desk. A skeleton standing with a scythe at the ready and wearing a crown, Rey had been a gift, intended to bring them good luck in their business. In his own office he dropped into his chair and eyed the other office tchotchke, a white plaster statue of Pollux standing with a horse—a gift from Pike.

On his phone he checked Svetlana's illicit tracking app for Conrad, his idiot cop ex-boyfriend. He was at his station, or at least his phone was. Conrad didn't actually know Slater could track him, but that was his own damn fault. It wasn't stalking, Slater told himself, because he needed to know where the guy was sometimes.

He dialed Conrad's cell and listened to it ring.

"I heard you bought a house," he said when he picked up.

"Yeah, it's a whole thing. Listen—I need you to run a plate for me."

"No," Conrad said.

"What do you mean, 'no'?" he demanded.

"I can't use police resources to help you with your business."

"That never stopped you before. Did you have an ethics training session this week or something?"

"Why not ask your business partner to do it?"

"I don't want to get too dependent on him," Slater said. "Plus he has to pay to pull the data. It doesn't cost you anything, and I'm already paying for it with my damn taxes."

Conrad sighed. "I just don't think it's a healthy pattern."

"You sound like a goddamn shrink right now. Listen to me: you'll do what I ask or I'll make your life a living hell."

"You already did that," he said, "and then we broke up."

"You broke us up," Slater snapped. "The way I remember it, my lifeless body got dumped in the gutter with a knife in my back."

"Doris says there's a guy."

"There's always a guy. Quit gossiping with her."

"She thought it might be serious. Like a forever-boyfriend type deal."

"I don't even know what it is," Slater said. "It's just starting."

"Is that why you bought the house?"

He took a breath. Conrad knew him so well. That's exactly why he'd bought the house. "You know, you're the only person who can see right through me."

"That's not so bad, is it? Having someone who knows you that well?"

"So are you going to run this plate," Slater said, "or am I going to come over there and punch you in the face?"

"Assault on a peace officer is a felony," he said flatly. "Text me the tag. I'll do it because I respect you, Slater. Not because you threatened me."

He ended the call and spent a minute texting him the Bronco's plate number. Idiot dick-smack Conrad. He had no idea what respect was.

Turning to his computer, he clicked the mouse to wake it up. He and Max had an account with a data broker that compiled hits from license-plate readers. Every cop car and tow truck and taxi was equipped with them now, meaning that everyone's anonymity on the roads was fading away. But the data was often useful.

They'd set it up for their business, and of course they had to pay for it, but otherwise they'd only had to attest on paper that they had a legitimate need for the data because they sometimes repo'd cars. That was a major variance from the truth, but apart from that low regulatory bar, no one cared.

Slater logged into the system and typed in the Bronco's plate number. There were over six hundred hits for the plate in the last few months. Once he'd paid for the list, it let him download a spreadsheet that contained all of them. One cell in each row showed the latitude and longitude of the sighting, and when he clicked on it, it was already set up to pull up a map. Going through the list was a bit laborious, with so many hundreds of rows, but at least he could sort them by zip code.

The vehicle had been spotted all over town, he saw as he got into it. Most often it was in Hollywood, near the freeway and Santa Monica Boulevard. If it really was Woody's car, that was near his house. Of course it could be his girlfriend's or his maid's ride. If lazy-ass Conrad would do his damn job, he'd already know who it was registered to.

The Bronco was also repeatedly scanned near Alsace Acres in Los Feliz, he found, as he got deeper into the list. Woody worked there—this had to be Woody's vehicle. Scrolling through more hits, another location that repeatedly came up was downtown, around Broadway and Seventh. That wasn't too revealing, as it was a dense part of town. Woody could be doing almost anything around there.

Enough work, he decided, and locked the computer with a keystroke. He had a hot man waiting, and dinner plans. Once he'd flicked off the office lights, and twisted his key in the deadbolt, he went around to the elevator. As he stood waiting his phone buzzed in his pants. It was a text from Conrad's cell:

The Bronco is registered to Woodrow Newkirk.

A second text had a street address in Hollywood—the place he'd already been today.

"Finally," he muttered, and tucked his phone away.

Hustling over to the parking lot, he drove back to Echo Park and nosed the Thunderbird into his garage. The new door rolled up faster than the original had, he realized. It wouldn't be as safe if some fructose-addled child were messing with it, but Svetlana knew he didn't have any kids, and that his priority would be expediency.

SEVEN

UPSTAIRS SLATER FOUND PIKE in the kitchen, leaning over the sink. He'd changed into long pants and a dress shirt, likely in preparation for meeting Doris. He was eating a nectarine like it was an apple, a dribble of juice visible on his chin, and he waved it in greeting. Slater stepped up and embraced him, and mouthed his chin, licking up the tart drops. Pulling back, he squeezed Pike's biceps.

"You're so beautiful," Slater said. "I can hardly stand it."

"You poor thing."

"I'm serious," he said intently, raising his voice. "I can't stand it."

Pike pulled him close, and kissed him, leaning into his body. Hands on his neck, then his head, exploring his mouth, still sweet with the fruit, Slater could feel his dick swelling in his jeans. The doorbell chimed, and he pulled back.

"Damn it. She's here already." Slater adjusted his crotch. "Steel yourself, son. It's go time."

He trotted down to the front door and pulled it open to find Doris and Conrad standing there, beaming at him. Petite and with some gray showing, Doris was dressed in capris and a billowy cotton blouse for the summer heat. Conrad had his dark hair in a natty style, his barrel-chested frame pleasingly clad in a tropical-print Hawaiian shirt. His SUV was parked at the curb, but Doris's Buick was nowhere in sight. That meant they'd come together.

Leaning in, he kissed Doris. "What's in the bag?"

She handed it to him. "It's just a candle. I didn't know what you needed."

Slater looked to Conrad and frowned. "It makes me nervous when a cop shows up banging on my door. I feel like you're going to make me empty my pockets."

"Innocent people don't need to be afraid of the police."

"That's what cops always say. Usually right before they slam you on the hood of a prowl car."

Doris looked past him and smiled. "You must be Pike."

Pike greeted her and stepped closer, then embraced her. That seemed a little forward, Slater thought.

Conrad introduced himself, and Pike said, "We've actually talked on the phone. I called you when I saw that flag in Slater's file."

"I remember," Conrad said, and flashed that goofy smile. "You're ATF."

"Why is there a flag in his file?" Doris said.

Slater waved an arm. "That's a very good question."

"It's no big deal," Conrad said. "It's just so I could explain what Slater had done in the Galliform situation."

That was an obfuscation, Slater knew. Conrad had flagged him in a lame attempt to keep him out of trouble.

"When you said plus-one," Slater said, eyeing Doris, "I thought you meant that old man who's been hanging around your place."

"Albert isn't that old," she said, and to Pike, "We've been dating for ages. He's a doctor. He said he had to work today, but I think he's actually afraid Slater might assault him."

"I'm glad to hear it," Slater said. "Maybe that'll keep him on good behavior."

Doris waved to the far side of the garage. "What's the other doorway for?"

"That's Grace's apartment."

"So are you going to let us in?" Conrad said.

Slater heaved a weary sigh but turned and led them upstairs, on the landing waving them into the bedrooms.

"Yours looks great," Doris said, "but the other one is empty. You need to get a bed for it. That way you can have guests."

"I don't want guests."

She shrugged. "You never know."

"I kind of like the minimalist vibe."

"What good is an empty room?" Doris said, and threw up a hand. "Just buy a bed."

"You think I'm made of money?"

"You did just buy a house twice the size of mine," she said.

Slater eyed Pike. "She just wants somewhere to warehouse her out-of-town relatives when there's a family wedding."

He led the way up to the top floor, and stood with them in the big open room.

"It's huge," Conrad said, hands on his hips. "And it's really beautiful. But you definitely need more furniture."

"It's so yang up here, isn't it?" Pike said. "All the open space and the light."

Doris stepped over to the French doors. "What did you pay?"

"Eight fifty," Slater said. "I put a third down."

"My son, the *macher*. That seems low for what it is."

"It is only two bedrooms."

"That's still a big mortgage," Conrad said. "You'll be paying for it for a while."

"Eight fifty?" Pike said. "Are you kidding me? In my neighborhood this might be worth three fifty. If there was a tailwind."

"I won't deny that this city has gone insane," Doris said. "What part of Albuquerque do you live in?"

"Corrales. Do you know that part of the world?"

"I don't."

"It's suburban," Pike said, "but the lots are big. I'm twenty minutes from downtown."

"Not like LA suburban," Slater said. "It's right on the river. He's got a stable and land for horses. It's more like the countryside."

"It sounds like arcadia," Doris said.

Pike chuckled. "I wish I had time for horses."

"Your neighbors would take care of them," Slater said. "He knows all his neighbors." Eyeing Pike, he added, "Weirdo."

"It's a good idea to connect with your neighbors," Conrad said. "You should meet them, at least, since you're new here."

"I gave that assignment to Grace," Slater said. "She knows how to play nice. She can butter up the chumps, draw up a sucker list, and we'll both get the gravy."

Conrad frowned. "You're treating your new home life like it's a con."

"She's a skilled operative. And it is a con—the same way that real estate is a con, and banking, and car insurance. They're all running a grift on me at this very moment, trying to suck me dry."

"Moving Grace over here was a mitzvah," Doris said.

Slater shrugged. "She is paying rent."

"Still, at that age having someone you trust nearby is huge." She gestured to the vases of flowers lining the walls. "This has to be about you, Pike. I can't imagine Slater buying cut flowers."

"It brightens up the place, doesn't it?" Pike said, and to Slater, "Do you want to offer your guests something to drink?"

"Good idea," Slater said. "I'll do it."

"I can see already that you're a civilizing force," Doris said.

"He just needs a reminder once in a while." Pike met her gaze. "The foundation is there—I know you brought him up right."

Doris followed Slater back to the kitchen. "He's quite the honey dripper," she said quietly.

"I'm sure he wants to make a good impression."

"So handsome too."

"That's what makes him dangerous." Slater pulled open the icebox. "I've got soda water, lemonade, or beer."

"It's too early for beer."

She helped him pour glasses of lemonade, and they carried them back toward the French doors.

"Has Slater told you about his court diversion experiences?" Conrad was saying to Pike.

"Experiences, plural? Not yet. That sounds intriguing."

Slater handed him a glass of lemonade. "I'm not sure you need to be gossiping about that, like a damn costermonger."

"I'm just laying out the facts," Conrad said. "No embellishments. I wouldn't want to bruise your fragile ego."

Slater jabbed a finger at him, formulating a retort, but the doorbell rang, and he caught himself. "That'll be Miguel." He handed Conrad his glass and walked toward the stairs.

"Who's Miguel?" Conrad called after him.

"The caterer."

When Slater opened the front door, he found Miguel, a squat guy with a buzzed head, peering over the stack of sealed foil trays in his arms. Greeting him, Slater took a couple of the trays and led the way up to the kitchen, where they set them on the counter.

"There's a few more things in the truck," Miguel said, and trotted back down the stairs.

Conrad stepped over to the kitchen. "That's pretty bougie, hiring a caterer for four people."

"The guy owes me a favor," Slater said. "His food is really good. His wife makes the tortillas herself."

"I remember your kitchen chops." He chuckled. "If you tried to cook, we'd be getting microwave burritos or burned toast."

Slater jutted his chin toward the French doors. Pike was leaning toward Doris, talking about something, his eyes bright. "Why did you leave those two alone?"

"You're worried about what kind of intel they're sharing."

Slater huffed, watching them. "I suppose it's inevitable they're going to talk."

"He seems really nice," Conrad said. "Authentic. Not like all the flakes floating around LA."

"Don't marry me off just yet. I hardly know him."

"Well, he's nice. You deserve nice, Slater."

Eyeing Conrad, he could feel his heart pounding. "I'm not so sure about that. I think he might be too good for me."

"That goes without saying."

"It's weird, right? I'm used to having nothing, nothing to worry about, a shitty little apartment where I drank powdered cowboy coffee. Now I've got a mortgage, and a coffeemaker, and a man."

"It's almost as if you're acting like an adult."

Miguel appeared again at the top of the stairs. "Hey, *patrón.*"

Slater stepped over, and saw he'd brought the warm tortillas folded in a cotton towel. Miguel spent a minute telling him about the food, and Slater pulled out his wad of cash, and handed over the requisite bills.

"Have you heard the name Chila before?" Slater said.

"That's short for Isidra," Miguel said, tucking the money away. "It's a woman's name."

"Is it common?"

"There's lots of Chilas around." He waved to the others across the room and called, "Enjoy."

Miguel headed down the stairs, and Pike and Doris walked over to inspect the food. Slater dug cutlery out of a drawer.

"All this is vegan?" Pike said.

"That's what Miguel specializes in," Slater said. "Plant-based Mexican. Pretentious Westsiders pay him the big bucks for a spread like this. They think that hiring him means they're tuned in to the vibe of the masses."

"It's so damn much food," Conrad said, scooping rice onto his plate. "What are you going to do with all this? Don't you just order one plate per person?"

"That's the most *goyishe* thing I've ever heard," Slater said flatly.

"What does being Jewish have to do with it?"

"You always want to have lots of food," Doris said. "The worst thing would be to let people go hungry."

Once she'd filled her plate, Doris nodded to the French doors. "Let's sit outside."

They followed her out onto the deck, and Pike pulled out a chair for her, balancing his plate in his other hand.

"You should sit here," he said. "It has the best view."

"I love that you can see downtown from here." Doris set her plate on the table.

"The top floors of the Financial District, at least," Slater said, taking the chair opposite.

After they'd eaten, Doris pushed her plate away. "So how did you two meet?"

Sated, Slater had slumped back in his chair, and gestured languorously. "Our passion was forged in the fiery depths of an interstate terrorism investigation. Pike's first caress felt like the heat of a million suns."

"That hardly sounds like hyperbole at all," she said, raising her eyebrows.

"It's actually kind of true," Pike said. "It was literally a million volts. He horned in on my case, so I tased him." He jabbed the air with his fork. "Zap."

"I wouldn't call that a romantic story," Doris said.

Conrad chuckled. "It's a great story, though."

"Calling our romance a 'story,'" Slater said, waggling his fingers to put air quotes around the word, "doesn't do it justice. Lo, there's so much more going on. On so many different levels. Our romance is a narrative complex. Like Jason and the Argonauts, or the Iliad, or the Oresteia of Aeschylus."

"Are you even sober right now?" Conrad said, his brow furrowing.

"As a judge." Slater pointed two fingers at his own eyes, then jabbed a finger at Conrad. "With the hot focus of a laser beam."

Pike laughed and set his fork down. "It's been intense."

"That's my son," Doris said.

"I was in a used bookstore a while back," Pike said, "and I found an old paperback about the Greek myths. Mostly from Ovid. We've been reading it to each other. Hence Slater's fluency with the Iliad and the Oresteia."

"Now, that's romantic." She eyed Slater. "I'm glad to hear you pick up a book once in a while."

Later on, Doris and Slater were cleaning up in the kitchen. Outside the sky was lit by the golden light of the end of the day. Conrad was still out on the deck, sharing something with Pike, and both of them guffawed.

"Damn it," Slater muttered, glancing toward them.

"To me that seems like a very good sign," Doris said. "They're being civil."

"If you say so."

She smiled. "You're really into this guy."

Slater leaned back on the counter. "He makes me want to be a better person. But it's all new. It feels like we're right at the start."

"A minute ago you compared your romance to the Iliad."

"That was partly for Conrad's benefit. But it's like Pike said: intense. It's been a while since I've been so emotional with a guy. Like a muscle I don't use much. I'm not completely familiar with it yet."

Doris pulled him into a tight embrace, then stepped back, tears in her eyes.

"What's with the waterworks?" he said, and frowned.

She reached up to brush his cheek with her thumb. "I'm happy for you."

EIGHT

AFTER CONRAD AND DORIS had gone, as twilight was fading outside, Slater flopped onto his bed.

When Pike walked in, he stretched out beside him. "Tired?"

"It's a lot, right? Doris is a handful."

"I love her."

"She seems to love you back."

Pike climbed up and straddled him. "Want to get busy?"

"About that," he said, and reached up to squeeze his arms. "I might have signed us up for a three-way later."

His brow furrowed. "Seriously?"

"Too much?" Slater said.

"Maybe not. Who with?"

"One of my operatives. A desk jockey. His name is Andy."

"You sleep with your operatives."

"I know it's stupid. Mostly I try to keep my dick out of my work."

"You're a very sexual person," Pike said.

"He's the one who's the sex maniac, orchestrating a three-way with someone he's never met." Slater raised his eyebrows. "He's kind of jealous of you."

"So why would you agree to a three-way? Is that some kind of LA thing?"

"It's an Andy thing. If he can get to know you a little, I think it'll calm him down."

"I guess I should be glad I can be of service." Pike chuckled. "When is this happening?"

"Later this evening. So we should save our sexual energy."

Pike slid off him and rolled onto his back. "I've been in the house too long. Take me somewhere that's quintessential LA."

"There's ten million people here. It's hard to pin down a typical experience. But there's a straight place I want to go that overlaps with my case."

"Do we have to act straight?" Pike said.

"Oh, hell, no."

"Is there a dress code?"

"What you're wearing is fine."

"So let's roll."

Slater groaned and forced himself to sit up.

It was cooler without the sun, and they climbed in the Thunderbird, and drove to Los Feliz, trolling for parking on the boulevard. Eventually Slater pulled into a space, and they walked back toward the nightclub.

"So what does this place have to do with your case?" Pike said, walking abreast.

"My target works here. I want to get an eye on him, and figure out what he's up to."

A dark red canopy stretched across the sidewalk, emblazoned in yellow with ALSACE, and they stepped through the door.

Inside, at the tall desk, the host was wearing a burgundy vest with a name tag, her hair in thick dreads with purple highlights. As she greeted them, Slater palmed a twenty and briefly flashed it to her.

"Is there a booth for us?" he said.

Menus tucked under her arm, she stepped out, and tapped Slater's hand, deftly retrieving the bill. "Of course. Follow me."

The big room had white vinyl booths around the sides and dining tables in the middle. At one wall was a low stage, with mike stands and a grand piano at the side.

The host set the menus down at a booth with a front-on view of the stage. As she stepped away, they slid onto the U-shaped bench.

"This is a great table," Pike said. "How much did you have to bribe her?"

"It wasn't a bribe. I tipped her. Twenty bucks."

"That feels like Vegas."

"Except this is real. This place has been here since before the war."

A guy who looked to be in his twenties stepped over, his black hair carefully coiffed, wearing the same burgundy vest as the host.

"What can I get you?"

"Beer, I think," Pike said.

"Go for the Kronenbourg," Slater said. "From the tap. Same for me. And bring us that vegan Cobb salad to share."

As the server stepped away, Pike said, "I don't hear that beer mentioned very often."

"It's from Alsace."

"Nothing about this place says Alsace except the name."

Slater eyed him sidelong. "And the Kronenbourg."

A few minutes later the server returned and set down their beer glasses. Slater handed him a C-note.

"You can settle up after," he said.

"In case we have to leave in a hurry."

He nodded and took the bill.

"Are you planning on leaving in a hurry?" Pike said.

"You never know. You need to stay nimble."

They both looked toward the stage when the lights went up, and a guy with a mike in hand stepped out. He had slicked-back hair and wore a black suit with a bow tie.

"Welcome, friends," he said, his voice amplified by the sound system. "It's nice to see you all here. For your pleasure this evening, we have that duo that you all know and love."

There was scattered applause, and as the MC stepped off, a spotlight struck the curtain, and a man and woman stepped out. He was wearing a dark suit with a black shirt, open at the neck, and had glaringly unnatural thick black hair. He sat at the piano and wriggled his fingers. The woman was much flashier, in a sequined black gown, her auburn mane styled to tumble behind her ears. She stood at one of the mikes.

"Hello, everyone," she said, her tone soft and mellow, and flashed a smile.

The pianist started to play, and after a few bars the woman launched into a song: "I don't know why but I'm feeling so sad / I long to try something I never had."

Pike sipped his beer and slid an arm around Slater's shoulder. "I love these two. She can actually pull off the torch. They must be octogenarians. Although with that rug, he could pass for eighteen."

"In his dreams," Slater said. "The songbird is Frances, and the ivory pounder is Danny. They've been doing this since I was a kid."

Pike chuckled. "You came to a nightclub as a kid?"

"Once in a while. Not at night, though. Doris liked the atmosphere, and she used to come swing dancing here on Sunday afternoon. You see where the floor is a different color?" He pointed toward the tables in front of the stage. "They'd move everything off the dance floor, and Doris would park me in a booth to do my homework. The deal we cut was that she could stay as long as she wanted if I could order as many snacks as I wanted."

He laughed. "You were a player even then."

A guy walked in from the lobby and stopped, and folded his arms, watching the musicians. His tight haircut in knobby twists, Slater could only see him in profile, but it was Woody, unmistakably. He was hotter than he'd expected, wearing a dark-blue jacket, the matching trousers cut to flatter his body. They had a dark stripe down the leg—it was the house band's uniform.

Slater sat up and spoke quietly. "That's my target."

"He doesn't necessarily look like a lowlife," Pike said, studying him.

Woody wasn't overly tall, but he had a presence, and took up space. A woman in the restaurant's vest stepped up to him, and stood abreast, both of them looking toward the musicians. Slater slid out of the booth and walked behind them. They were standing close to the servers' supply stand, so he paused there and picked up a menu. Facing away from them, he gazed absently at it and tried to listen in.

"I get the thing about tradition," Woody said, "but you have to admit, it's kind of dead-ass."

"Everyone loves these two," the woman said. "That's why they come."

"You should give the band more time. And me. We're way more fun. We'd attract a lot more eyeballs than these two."

"The boss says they're off-limits," she said. "Save your floor show for Greenleaf."

Woody scoffed and turned to walk back toward the lobby.

As Slater replaced the menu, the server stepped up.

"Your Cobb salad will be right out," he said. "Can I get you something else?"

"I don't think so," Slater said. "When does the house band perform?"

"Soon. There's a break after Danny and Frances, and then they go on."

As he walked back to the booth to rejoin Pike, he pulled out his phone and typed a note with the name he'd overheard: Greenleaf. Tucking it away, he slid into the booth and sipped his beer.

"Are you going to talk to him?" Pike said.

"I really just wanted to see who he was, and what he was doing. I'm not sure if he's a gangster."

"Lots of nightclubs have syndicate entanglements, but superficially, he doesn't look like that to me."

That was actually a good insight, Slater realized. Pike dealt with more lowlifes than he did, and unlike Slater, the feds weren't afraid to go after gangsters.

Danny and Frances started into another song, and the food arrived, and they both munched on it. Slater's phone buzzed in his jeans, and he pulled it out. It was a text from Andy:

Your friend Isidra doesn't actually work for Westside Title Guarantee. Not anymore. Her job title was listed as "clerk," but she left that job a month ago.

Slater typed a reply:

Are you sure about the date? Did you talk to someone there?

Andy's response came a minute later:

> I saw her unemployment claim. It has the severance
> date on it.

That meant Chila got fired, Slater knew. You can't get unemployment if you quit. And that had happened well before she came to talk to Slater.

"Fucking royal fuck."

"Problem?" Pike said, setting his fork down.

"My client is lying to me. I don't know why she really wants to find this guy."

"What was her story?"

"She said she had an insurance payout for him. But I just found out she doesn't work in that field anymore."

"She's using you as a bird dog," Pike said.

"That means whatever the real reason is, she knows I wouldn't work for her on those terms."

"Maybe it's a grudge. She wants to break his kneecaps."

"She's not a gangster either," Slater said. "She worked in mortgage insurance."

"Is it a personal beef? Boy-girl problems. How old is she?"

"She's got a decade or so on this guy." Slater took a slurp of his beer. "I shouldn't be so pissed. People lie to me all the time. She's just another grifter."

Danny was on his feet now, and he and Frances both gave a little bow, to a round of applause. As they walked off, the stage went dark, and once the applause had faded, a chubby guy dressed in black stepped out and started setting up music stands.

Their server stepped up. "Another round?"

"Hit me," Slater said, and Pike assented too.

Soon the house band filed onto the stage, without introduction. There were eight of them, brass and strings and drums, even a pianist, and once they were settled in, the lights went up. Woody stepped onto the stage, and took hold of the mike that was positioned up front, and adjusted its height.

"At least he's not the drummer," Pike said.

"Why is that important?"

"Anyone I've ever met who was in a band says that drummers are nuts."

The music started, a lively jazz tune. Woody was right—they definitely brought more volume and more energy than Danny and Frances. Eventually Woody sang, his voice deeper than it had been in conversation: "We meet / and the angels sing / the angels sing the sweetest song I've ever heard."

"The man has great pipes," Pike said.

At the end of the song, they applauded along with the rest of the room. The response was marginally more enthusiastic than for Danny and Frances.

As Woody started into his next song, a guy walked in front of their booth. Lanky, with his black hair slicked back, he was wearing a stretchy black top and red jeans. He glanced at them, then did a double-take, and stopped.

"Slater," he said, his voice singsong.

Pointing a finger at him, it took Slater a second to retrieve his name. "Jack."

"What are you doing here?"

"Trying to have a drink in peace, and listen to some music."

"Nice." Jack nodded. "I live right up the block."

"I know. I've been there."

"Who's your hot arm candy?"

"The name is Pike," he said, and extended a hand, flashing that easy smile.

Jack grasped it with three fingers and gave it a delicate shake. Slater had to stifle a groan. Why had he done that? It was like an invitation. Sure enough, Jack set his highball on the table, and slid in next to Pike, and touched his forearm.

"I come in here all the time," Jack said. "Did you see Danny and Frances?"

Pike nodded. "They're old-school."

"And also just old. They actually needed to take their fiber supplement and their evening pills and get to bed." Jack nodded to the stage. "This is the house band."

"Do you know the tired canary?" Slater said.

"I never met him, but I know his name is Woody Newkirk."

"What makes him tired?" Pike said, eyeing Slater.

"Doesn't he look like he's about to fall asleep?"

"He looks like he's making love to everyone in the room with his eyes," Pike said. "This stuff is classic, and he's really bringing it."

"Slater's right, though," Jack said. "I think this genre might actually induce depression. Good music has a beat, and you can dance to it. Usually it comes out of a computer, not a bunch of guys in matching suits."

"Preach," Slater said.

Pike laughed. "So the only good music is dance music. Who knew?"

"You two are sitting awfully close," Jack said. "That tells me you're on a date."

"We are on a date," Pike said.

"Hubba hubba. I can't believe Slater has a boyfriend. A specific one, I mean."

Pike raised his eyebrows. "That implies that Slater sleeps around."

"Hey." Slater frowned and shot him a look.

"I always thought program would be perfect for you," Jack said.

"You mean AA?" Pike said.

"Maybe that one too, but there's one for gay guys who are addicted to hookups. It's called Sexual Compulsives Anonymous."

"Quit gossiping about my sex life," Slater demanded. "I'm not an addict."

Jack held up his palms in mock surrender, then eyed Pike. "So where are you from?"

"Is it that obvious that I'm not local?"

Jack cocked his head, and sipped at the straw in his drink, looking him over. "It's the clothes, maybe. And the haircut."

"Jack is in the image business," Slater said. "He knows clothes and hair and makeup."

"I'm a stylist. Makeup is my bread and butter. For fun I do drag—my alter ego is Miss Mercy Days."

Pike laughed. "She sounds like fun."

"You should come see her," Jack said. "I'm on stage at a place in Hollywood next week. How long are you in town for?"

"Slater's going to drop me at the airport in the morning."

"Aw." He frowned, and made pouty lips. "Which one?"

"LAX this time."

Jack inhaled sharply, and flattened a palm on the table, and recoiled, his eyes wide in mock astonishment. "So it's serious." He reached for Pike's left hand. "I don't see a ring on that finger."

"What are you talking about?" Pike said.

"A good friend will drive you to the airport in Burbank, or even Long Beach, but only someone who truly loves you would drive you to LAX."

"Good to know." Pike nodded. "I love your eye makeup, Jack."

"It's subtle, right? It's Thursday, not Mardi Gras." Jack slapped his forearm. "I could do yours."

"Do you think I need it?"

"Honey, everyone needs it." Jack dug in his bag and produced a stubby black pencil.

"Just go easy," Slater said.

Taking hold of Pike's chin, Jack adjusted the position of his head, and leaned in.

"Don't move," he said, and delicately applied the pencil to his lower eyelids.

When Jack pulled back, Pike said, "How does it look?"

"I'm not finished yet." Jack scrabbled in his bag and found a mascara brush. Shifting Pike's chin again, he set to work. "You have perfect lashes."

"Is this stuff waterproof?" Pike said.

"It's not. So Slater, do not make him cry." A moment later Jack snapped the brush closed and sat back. "Now you're perfect."

Pike turned to Slater. "Better?"

"It's actually subtle," Slater said. "You were fuckable before. Now you're fuckable plus your eyes really pop."

"My work here is through," Jack said, and held a thumb to his ear, his pinkie to his cheek. "Call me."

Once he'd gone, Pike said, "I wish they all could be California boys."

"That specific boy is a pistol," Slater said.

"Based on his taste in music, I take it he's a club rat."

"At least he wasn't tweaking."

"If he had been, I wouldn't have let him sit down."

The band was still on, without Woody, playing an instrumental.

"I've seen enough," Slater said. "Do you want to bug out?"

NINE

IKE AND SLATER SLID out of the booth and walked out to the lobby. On the way up the block to his car, Pike wrapped an arm around his waist. It felt so good, and Slater's heart was pounding just from the guy's touch. Everything about it was exactly right. Why was he so enamored with this, the proximity, the warmth of his skin?

Once they were in the Thunderbird, Slater started the engine and pulled into the street, then cruised onto the side street, and onto the next block.

"This neighborhood is really old," he said. "Lots of apartments with no parking. Everybody has to street park."

"Are you looking for something?" Pike said.

"That." Slater nodded to a parked car as he braked and then pulled out his phone.

"The Bronco? Whose is it?"

"It might be Woody's." The plate number matched, Slater saw, and he pulled ahead a few feet, paralleling the vehicle.

"Your target," Pike said.

Reaching into the backseat, Slater grabbed a pair of black latex gloves from the box he kept there and wriggled into them. "I'll be right back."

Climbing out, he opened the trunk and retrieved one of his vehicle trackers. The black plastic housing was the size of a cell phone, but thicker, and it had metal ribs on one side to adhere to steel. He wiped it down on his shirt. There was nothing he could do about the traces of his DNA on it, but he didn't need to make it easy by leaving his prints too, in the unlikely event someone found it.

Examining it, he found the recessed power switch, and clicked it on with a latex-clad fingernail. He stepped around to the Bronco's rear wheel and squatted there, blocked from view by the Thunderbird, and reached up inside the well. It took a minute for the magnetic ribs to find purchase, and he shifted the device around, but eventually he felt the satisfying tug of it snapping on.

Svetlana built this model to use Wi-Fi and cell signals to calculate a general location, so it didn't need a view of the sky. It used a lot less power because the panoply of Wi-Fi stations were much stronger than GPS from space, so the battery would last for almost a week.

As he rose, he noticed Pike watching him in the side mirror, his brow furrowed. He peeled off his gloves and got behind the wheel, tossing them on the floor of the backseat.

"You did not just do what I think you did," Pike said, eyeing him in the dim light.

"Of course not. I thought I saw a stray cat. I was going to rescue it, but it must have run away." He shifted into Drive and headed up the block.

"Oh, Slater, come on. I did exactly the same thing to the vehicle you were driving in Voirrey's Corner."

"You tried to rescue a cat?"

"You know what I'm talking about."

"Think about your plausible deniability. I'm not doing anything wrong. You don't have to worry about it."

Pike huffed and was quiet for a while, looking out the window. Slater turned onto Sunset, headed east.

"Not my circus, not my monkeys," he said finally.

"There you go."

Sunset was moving fairly well, as usual punctuated by lots of red lights.

"Where does your operative live?" Pike said.

"Downtown."

"Is there anything I need to know about him?"

"His name is Andy," Slater said, "and he's a no-bullshit kind of guy. If he wants you to know something, he'll tell you."

He parked in the surface lot behind Andy's building, and paid the attendant the flat evening rate. Once they were off the elevator, and walking up to Andy's door, Slater took a deep breath.

"You're nervous about this," Pike said.

"Maybe a little."

"I watched you go after an armed fugitive at full gallop, and you're worried about a three-way with people you already know?"

"It's about the sticky stuff. Interpersonal relationships. That's way harder to predict than what a lowlife is going to do."

When Andy pulled open his door, he was clad in his usual boxer shorts and a T-shirt, and Slater introduced them.

Andy gave Pike a pointed once over. "Come in."

"This is a great apartment," Pike said, looking around.

"I know it's … small, but it suits me."

Pike tapped the handlebars of Andy's red mobility scooter, parked next to the wall. "Sweet ride."

"It's easier than taking cars everywhere. My … maximum range on foot is about six blocks."

"You've got CP?"

Andy frowned. "Slater didn't tell you that?" He looked at Slater. "Why didn't you … tell him that?" he demanded.

Slater put his hands on his hips. "Because it doesn't fucking matter."

"It matters to me. It's kind of a … defining characteristic of my life."

"Don't get pissed at me," Slater snapped.

Andy jabbed a finger at him. "Settle down."

"I work with a guy who has CP," Pike said, loud enough that they both turned to him. "He has the exact same input gauntlets." He gestured to Andy's desk. "He can type faster than anyone in the office."

"He sounds like a … prizewinner," Andy said flatly.

Pike jutted his chin. "He's not nearly as hot as you, though."

"At least your vision is in order," Andy said, his tone softening, and chuckled.

"Enough with the chin music," Slater said. "You're the stage director. Tell us what to do."

"You can do whatever you want, as long as I'm the focus." He thumped his fist on his chest.

"I can work with that." Slater sat on the side of the bed and started to untie his boots.

Andy dropped his shorts, and pulled off his shirt, and climbed on beside him, then eyed Pike, who stood next to the desk, watching them, unmoving. "Clothes off, son. Make it snappy."

Pike grinned and unbuttoned his shirt, then slid off his chinos, and walked around to the other side of the bed. As he lay down, Andy grabbed his cock, eliciting a gasp.

"I like this," Andy said, stroking him for a moment.

Once Slater was naked, he shifted next to Andy, and kissed his neck, and caressed his chest, and squeezed his cock, already hard. Pike leaned in and met Andy's mouth, and Slater moved in for a three-way kiss. It was exhilarating, tasting both of them, and intense, exploring their mouths. He felt his cock swelling.

Andy pulled back and grabbed his own cock, rock-hard now. "One of you, suck my dick."

Pike shifted down and took him into his mouth, and Andy closed his eyes, moaning at the sensation. Slater sat up to reach for Pike's cock, but Andy slapped his hand.

"This is about me."

Lying back, Slater pushed his arm under Andy's neck, and ravished him, mouthing his jaw, and his neck, and his ear, running a hand over his chest. Shifting closer, he draped his shin over Andy's legs so that a random muscle spasm wouldn't give Pike a black eye.

"Enough," Andy said. "I'm going to fuck Slater. Pike, I want you facing me."

Slater reached under the side of the bed and grabbed a condom, then climbed over Andy and stretched out between them. Ripping it open, he took a minute to roll it onto Andy, and lube him up.

"What do you want me to do?" Pike said, stroking himself.

"You need to look at me."

On his side, Slater reached back and guided Andy's rock-hard cock with his hand. He had to do most of the maneuvering, and he gasped as Andy penetrated him, and winced at the intensity as he pressed hard. That wasn't about lax muscle control—he was being rough with him on purpose.

Andy started thrusting slowly, and when Pike grabbed Slater's cock, he said, "Look at me, not at him."

Pike shifted closer and kept his eyes on Andy. With his arm stretched behind him, Slater had his fingers spread wide on Andy's butt, stabilizing his thrusts. Pike started to stroke himself and Slater together, and Slater soon got hard again. Andy built up to pounding him, his whole body thrashing, and he climaxed with a yelp. Slater met Pike's mouth and came, and Pike quickly followed, moaning and straining into him.

Pike pulled away, and Slater twisted onto his back, panting. He folded an arm under Andy's neck, and briefly kissed him, then sank into the bed.

Once he'd caught his breath, and his muscle movements had slowed, Andy sat up on his elbows. "You can shower, if you want."

"Why would I do that?" Pike said. "I'm so content right now."

"I messed up your guy-liner," Andy said. "You look like a racoon."

Pike chuckled and wiped at his cheek. "No great loss."

"Do you wear it every day?"

"I don't. It seems like that would be a lot of work."

"We've got an early morning," Slater said, and sat up.

Soon both of them were dressed, with Andy watching them, still naked, propped up on his pillows.

When they were ready to leave, Pike said, "Thank you for inviting me."

"Such good manners." Andy chuckled. "I'm glad I got to meet you."

Spent but sated when they climbed into his car, Slater started the engine and pulled into the street.

Pike leaned back on the headrest. "Well, he seems nice."

Slater scoffed. "He was being a total fucking prick tonight. But maybe he's working through his stuff. The thing about being pissed at me."

They were both quiet as Slater accelerated onto the freeway, Pike gazing out the side window as the dark city rolled by.

Eventually Pike spoke. "Maybe what we've got really is a narrative complex."

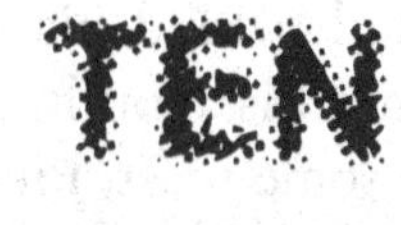

WHEN SLATER WOKE, PIKE was sitting up next to him in bed. In that unflattering position his pecs looked soft, and flabby, but still somehow perfect, because it was him. Slater shifted closer and caressed his chest.

"'Turkey in the Straw,'" Pike said.

"What?"

"The tune the ice cream truck is playing. It's been parked up the block for a while now. Like your friend Jack said, it's got a good beat, and you can dance to it. The one that comes by my mom's house plays 'Pop Goes the Weasel.'"

"I get it. Those are both rock-solid ice cream songs."

"I just looked it up. In the 1850s it was a world-wide dance craze."

Slater chuckled. "'Turkey in the Straw'?"

"No—that weasel tune."

He climbed up on Pike and ground his morning hard-on into his belly. "I'll make your weasel pop, wise guy. I can't believe you're focused on that."

"It woke me up."

"Can you get your hands on one of those Javelin missile launchers? I could solve the neighborhood noise pollution problem in very short order."

Pike put a hand behind his neck, and pulled him down, and met his mouth. After they'd had quick sex, and ate some toast, Pike carried his bag down the stairs, and loaded it into the backseat of the Thunderbird. The trip to LAX was quiet, both of them somber at the looming separation. Slater navigated to the right terminal, and pulled up to the curb, and shifted into Park.

"Truth time." Pike took a breath. "I think I'm falling for you, Ibáñez. It's more than just infatuation. Like maybe I'm in love with you."

"I'm kind of getting there too."

Pike laughed, his tone deep and rich, and leaned over to kiss him.

"I guess I should say it, huh," Slater said.

"There's no rules. Those LA people on reality TV shows say, 'Love you; mean it.'"

"That means they actually don't. Or maybe only a fraction, like, 'I love you two-fifths of a full amount.'"

"This is such a singular town," Pike said.

He met his gaze. "It's true, though. I love you." He put his palm on Pike's face. "You know I mean it. You drive me freaking crazy."

"In a good way?"

"The best possible way. It makes my stomach hurt sometimes. I can't think straight anymore."

After a last lingering kiss, Pike climbed out, and retrieved his bag. Slater watched him drag it inside, through the terminal doors and out of view, a firm lump in his throat.

It wasn't busy here, with no curb cops to shoo him away, and he took a deep breath, and dug out his phone, and checked the tracker on Woody's car. It was functioning, like Svetlana's stuff always did, the green location circle on the map imprecise and encompassing a couple of houses. But he knew that street, recognized it without even zooming in—one of the houses was Woody's. The Bronco was parked at his place in Hollywood.

Slater nosed into the traffic, and got on the 105, and went back downtown, pulling into the surface lot across from his office. When he got upstairs, Etta was at the front desk, using the computer. The little statue of Rey Pascual was turned to face her now, Rey's bony empty eye sockets watching her work. When she wasn't here she rotated it to face the entrance, as if he were guarding it.

"Are you working with Max today?" Slater said as he stepped in.

Etta sat back in her chair. "That's the plan. He'll be in soon."

He put his hands on his hips. "Isn't it a school day?"

"It's actually one of our student-free days. I'm all caught up on professional development, so I ducked out."

"You get a lot of free time. It seems like a great job."

"Except that the pay is garbage." Her expression brightened. "Listen, I loved Pike."

"Hey—I saw him first."

She chuckled. "You know what I mean. He's kind of perfect for you."

"You think? It's hard for me to be objective. I'm kind of lost in it right now. Lost in him."

"Well, he's into you too, in case you were wondering. I saw the way he looks at you."

"I took him to LAX this morning. We used the *l* word."

"Nice," she said emphatically. "Max is afraid you're going to move to Albuquerque and bust up the business."

"That's never going to happen. If I left this town for more than a few days, I'd wither and dry up and blow away."

He stepped into his office and eyed the statue of Pollux on his desk. Its counterpart, a matching statue of Castor, was on Pike's desk in Albuquerque. The little guy didn't really look like him, or like Pike, but he had great hair. Pike. He couldn't even begin to think about moving in with the guy. That was crazy talk.

Pulling his attention away from Pollux, he heaved his boots up onto his desk and pulled his keyboard into his lap. He did a search online for the word he overheard the woman at Alsace Acres say to Woody: Greenleaf. There were lots of people with that name, he found, scrolling through the results, and then a news item came up, titled "Renovations Near Completion at Greenleaf."

It wasn't news, he realized, but a press release styled to sound like news. Greenleaf was a nightclub, opening soon, upstairs from the old Sackett's cafeteria. Slater knew that place—like Alsace Acres, Sackett's was a classic, and it had been there forever.

The article didn't give an opening date, but it talked about the care that club promoter Les James had taken to restore the fixtures and finishes of the original nightclub. It didn't mention Woody, or the planned entertainment, but if Les had restored the place to an earlier incarnation, maybe he'd have a band, like Alsace did.

He pulled up the list of license-plate-reader hits for Woody's car that he'd bought and looked for the ones downtown. Almost all of them were at the same coordinates—a parking structure that was right across the street from Sackett's. This had to be the Greenleaf that Woody was talking about—his car was parked there all the time. It had to be connected to him.

Locking his computer, he got up, and said good-bye to Etta, and headed down to his car. Seventh Street wasn't far, but there was no street parking around here, and he turned into the garage where Woody had parked.

There was a lot of foot traffic on Seventh, he saw, stepping out onto the sidewalk. As he crossed the street he had vague memories of walking into Sackett's with Doris and his father. Pushing a fiberglass tray along the track lining the narrow walkway next to the wall, ogling the steam tables. Mixed peas and carrots cut in little cubes, and a woman in a mint-green uniform, serving mashed potatoes with an ice cream scoop.

The place had to be a hundred years old, but inside it had been renovated, he saw. It was still a cafeteria, but the floor plan was more open, and it looked more upscale now. He walked through to the dining room. This hadn't changed at all. It had a forest theme, the tables interspersed with a mix of cedars and pines and firs with the bark still on the logs, lining the walls, stretching to the ceiling that was painted like evergreen branches. As a kid he hadn't recognized how improbable this faux forest was. Those species needed different conditions. They'd never grow in such close proximity.

Slater climbed the staircase at the side, ascending to another dining room with a much lower ceiling. Here there was no decoration and fewer people at the tables. The stairwell that led up to the next floor had a chain across it, with a metal sign attached that said CLOSED. That's where Greenleaf had to be.

Stepping over the chain, Slater climbed the stairs. He didn't remember ever coming up this far. It was a sprawling open room, broken only by regular wood-paneled columns. There were some tables farther back, but near the stairs was the bandstand, fronted by a hardwood parquet floor for dancing. A lengthy bar ran along the far side. There was so much wood, some of it intricately carved; that all had to be original.

The bandstand was an alcove, he saw as he stepped toward it, with powder-blue walls that stretched onto the coved ceiling. That looked period too. Even the music stands were antiques, except for the logo attached to the fronts that read GREENLEAF.

Opposite the bar was a row of windows, showing the arched tops of the exterior stonework that faced Broadway. One window was filled with the back of a neon sign, lit up in that distinctive orangey-red even though it was midday. Moving closer, he could hear the soft buzzing of the transformer. The sign was facing outward but as he approached he could parse the backward script: DANCING.

Behind him, a voice spoke. "Are you from the distributor?"

Slater turned to find a woman approaching from the direction of the bar, her dark hair bundled back, wearing jeans. She had to be pushing fifty.

"What, now?" he said.

She stopped a few feet away. "I'm waiting on the liquor distributor."

"That's not me."

"Well, if you came to see the neon, you've seen it. You can get a better look at it from the sidewalk across the street."

Slater frowned. "Why do you think I'd want to look at a neon sign?"

She waved a hand. "It's famous."

He glanced at it again. "Are you sure about that?"

"When we pulled down the wallboard, we

found it," she said, stepping closer, "right where it is now, still plugged in and lit up. Sometime in the 1940s they boarded over the windows. On the outside too they put up aluminum cladding that completely obscured it. We just pulled it all down this spring. For eighty years that sign was switched on and inside the wall."

"Burning bright but unseen," Slater said. "That is a great story."

"Since we started the restoration work, we get looky-loos from the architectural society." She raised her eyebrows. "The chain across the bottom of the stairs is supposed to discourage that."

"How long has it been since this was a nightclub?"

"The original closed in 1964, but after that it operated as a bar off and on." She waved a hand. "Listen, son, I'm busy. I'm not giving tours."

"What about the guy who did all this?" Slater squinted as he tried to remember the name. "This is his place."

"What guy?"

He snapped his fingers. "Les James. When will he be in?"

"Les is a she, and she's actually here right now. You're looking at her."

"Got it." He nodded. "How do you hire your musicians?"

Her eyes narrowed. "I'm not hiring. That's all set up already. What do you play?"

"I don't actually need a job," he said. "When does the nightclub open?"

"We're doing a soft opening tomorrow. Tell your friends." She gestured toward the stairs. "Bye, now."

Slater trotted down, and back to his car, and drove the few blocks to the Financial District, where he parked in the garage under Della's office building. When he got up to her floor, Crystal was on the front desk.

She looked up and scowled at him. "She's at lunch."

"I'm here to see you."

"I don't need any more of your invective," Crystal said, leaning back in her chair, "and I definitely don't need to be seen consorting with a ruffian."

"You say that like you're not cut from exactly the same cloth." He dropped into the chair next to her desk. "How do you feel about field work?"

"I don't do that."

"But you can do it. I know you know how. I need you to get close to a guy."

"You want to use me as bait?" She shook her head. "That's not going to happen."

"I've seen you summon hospitality skills when it suited you," Slater said. "You don't have to sleep with him. Just flirt with him in the nightclub where he works."

"You actually want me to put on a hoochie dress and act like I'm a college student?"

"It's not that kind of nightclub. Do you know Alsace Acres? There's no dancing. You can dress like you did at that reception upstairs."

"So you don't need raunchy." Crystal looked

thoughtful. "You'd have to pay me."

"Of course."

"When?"

"Tonight."

"I don't know." She raised her eyebrows. "I'm on my period."

"So what?" Slater demanded. "You think Harriet Tubman shut down the underground railroad because she was feeling puffy and bloated? Or Amelia Earhart stopped flying? 'I'm just going to hang out on this atoll for a few days and listen to depressing folk music.' Take some damn ibuprofen."

"You have no idea what it's like to be a woman."

"I can't deny that. But I know when Aunt Flo visits, you want it both ways: 'Cut me some slack,' but 'Don't you dare treat me like I'm in any way incapacitated.'"

"Personally, I don't see that as a contradiction."

Slater threw up his hands.

"So what do you need to know from this guy?" she said.

Once he'd given her the rundown, he showed her photos of Woody.

"What's it going to cost me?" Slater said.

"A job like this?" Crystal pursed her lips for a moment. "Let's say five dollars."

He'd expected her to ask for double that, even fifteen hundred, but he frowned, and nodded thoughtfully. "I guess I can swing that. If you manage to talk to him."

"You'll pay me whether I find your target or not."

"Fine," he said, and frowned. "I'll meet you at Alsace Acres."

"If I'm dressing up, no way am I driving. You'll chauffeur me."

Once he'd typed her address into his phone, Slater went down to the Thunderbird, and started the engine, and checked the dashboard clock. There was enough time to work on his landscaping.

Up on the street, he navigated to the freeway, and headed to a nursery in Cypress Park. Inside he walked the edges of the big yard, looking over the shade plants. These places always gave him a buzz, seeing all the species and cultivars, thinking about all the possibilities. It reminded him that the world was so ripe with potential.

When he found the hydrangeas, sitting on a pallet in black plastic pots, he checked on the roots, and picked out three healthy ones, then paid for them and carried them out to his car, setting them on the floor of the passenger side. He felt a little guilty planting water-hogging stuff like this. If it were just for him, he'd plant dryland natives, but Grace's apartment had access to the little patch of backyard. He wanted her to enjoy it, and hydrangeas bloomed a lot.

Cruising back to his own neighborhood, he pulled into the garage and left the door up. Pulling on a pair of work gloves, he grabbed a spade from the wall rack, and some other tools, then lifted the pots with the plants out of his car.

There was a gate next to Grace's door that had access to the backyard, but he wanted to tell her what he'd be doing first, as he'd be working right outside her windows. He set the plants and the tools in front of it and then rang her bell.

A minute later Grace pulled open her door. Her hair was a white cloud, and when she smiled to greet him the lines deepened around her rheumy blue eyes.

"I'm going to do some planting in the back," Slater said, "and set up a drip line. It shouldn't take me long."

"Knock yourself out, dear. It's your house."

"How are you settling in?"

"I love this place, and I adore that little yard. It's a shame you don't get to use it. You can if you want to."

"I have that deck on the roof," Slater said. "That's enough outdoor space for me. Just let me know when the yard needs work, or if the plantings start to look parched."

"My girlfriends said I should take up gardening now."

"Fine by me. I have all the tools you'll need."

"You really should let me pay rent," Grace said. "You know I have the means."

"I'm just worried that if I get taken out, you'll be homeless, and I'm the one who dragged you out of a stable rent-controlled situation. You'll have to go back to paying insane market rates."

"I was already paying plenty in Westlake."

"Well, save your money for those contingencies," Slater said.

She furrowed her brow. "I'd say the trick is not

to get taken out. You have to be smart. Stay on your toes, and mitigate the risks."

"I know that's good advice. I'm not actually planning on taking the long sleep."

"If I had a man like your Mr. Pike coming around, I wouldn't either."

Slater grinned. "He's something else, isn't he?"

"A pure dreamboat. John Law never looked so good."

"That makes him dangerous, doesn't it?"

"Oh, honey—a rattlesnake in spit-polished oxfords." She shook her head. "Is he on the square with whatever agency he works for?"

"I think so."

Grace shrugged. "Well, an honest man isn't the worst thing. Just remember, if he has to choose between you and his oath, it might not go the way you hope."

ELEVEN

ONCE GRACE HAD GONE back inside, Slater went to the side gate and carried the pots and tools into the backyard. Grace had the wisdom of generations, and he knew she was right. He shouldn't have let Pike watch him plant that tracker on Woody's car. The way he felt about the guy was like a flash flood in the desert—it would hardly be raining at all, and suddenly you're overwhelmed by a raging torrent of muddy water. Slater was acting like he was distracted, or drunk, or high. The thing with Pike impaired his judgment. He needed to be smarter about it.

Looking around the space, it was mostly shaded, but there was room for a patio table. He'd have to get one of those for Grace. Her kitchen door was right here—she could have breakfast alfresco. The previous owners had planted Baja spurge on two sides as the privacy hedge. It was a reasonable choice, as it didn't hog up the water and it bloomed for months on end. After that initial insight they'd neglected this space, and it was mostly weeds and bare earth. But the soil was still good.

Only one side of the yard would get the morning sun that hydrangeas liked, and he spent time digging into the earth with the spade. Once the holes were big enough for the plants, he dug a trench over to the spigot for the drip line, and ran the hose, and buried it. He pulled the hydrangeas out of their pots, and massaged the earth around their roots, and set them in the ground, filling in around them with loose earth, and then tamped in a few handfuls of fertilizer with his fingers.

After he'd watered everything down, he coiled up the hose and set up the controller for the drip system. He'd check on it again in a week or so but hopefully he wouldn't have to mess with it very often. Taking a last look at the space, he realized it was still a little bare, even once the new plantings filled out. He'd have to put in some more ornamentals.

He carried the tools around to the garage, and stowed them, then went upstairs to wash up. It was time to roll, he realized, glancing at his phone. He changed into a clean shirt, dark green with a collar, then put Crystal's address into the navigation app.

The roads through downtown were a slow crawl to West Adams, and when he pulled up at the place, he found a stately house with classic porch pillars. Nineteenth century, probably, as there were lots of those in this neighborhood, one of the earliest moneyed suburbs. The house had been updated, with new siding and paint, and the drought-tolerant plantings in the yard were contemporary and well-tended. Somebody here had money.

A low fence ran along the sidewalk, and the gate was closed. Instead of walking up and knocking, he texted her:

I'm outside.

Crystal's reply came soon after:

Two minutes.

Slater climbed out of the car and stretched, then leaned on the front fender on the passenger side, facing the house. Daylight was fading, and he picked up the scent of night-blooming jasmine. He looked around but the plant wasn't in view. Maybe it was drifting from the next yard.

It took more like fifteen minutes, but finally Crystal appeared, in a chic blue dress that flattered her figure. Her hair was styled up, and jewelry glittered at her ears and her neck. Carrying a little black clutch, she was wearing heels, but they weren't so high that she couldn't walk.

"I was about to start honking the horn," Slater said.

She scowled at him. "Relax."

He pulled open the little gate for her. "I've never seen you up close in evening makeup. You look like a million bucks."

"I know," she said, her tone irritated. "It takes a lot of work to get to this point. And that requires patience from men and other people."

Slater opened the passenger door for her, and gently closed it once she'd climbed in. He got in behind the wheel and started the engine.

"I hope none of the neighbors saw me getting into this jalopy," Crystal said, as he pulled away from the curb.

"Don't be saying the *j* word. This is a classic, and it's cherry. I can't believe you live in that bougie house."

"I don't. I'm in the garden apartment around back."

Slater turned onto Vermont as the last bit of twilight was fading in the western sky.

"So you want me to seduce this Woody guy," Crystal said.

"You don't have to give him a hand job," he said. "Just chat with him. Buy him a drink or something."

"And you want to know if he's a lowlife."

"Or what his game is. On the surface he's just a musician, a vocalist with the house band, but I know he has money. What's under the gravy? Is he mixed up with the syndicate, or is he running some kind of game, or is he really a civilian?"

"It shouldn't be hard to figure out," she said, "especially if he's with the syndicate. Those guys have a very specific demeanor. If he's an outsider who's doing business with the syndicate, mention-ing that word will elicit a very specific reaction."

He glanced at her. It was impressive that she didn't need clarification—she knew exactly what he meant. Crystal had been a sheriff's deputy, he knew, and clearly she understood the cesspool, the dank underbelly of this town, down below the civilized world.

"Are you going to be hovering?" she said.

"The band doesn't go on until later, but musicians always show up way early. Woody will be in the green room and maybe in the dining room. I saw him there before. I'll hang out in the bar. You can come get me if you need me."

Pulling up at Alsace Acres, Slater stopped at the curb in front of the red awning. A few smokers were hanging around out front. He shifted into park and waited for her to climb out.

"You have to open the door for me," she said.

"What, are you disabled now?"

"I'm staying in character. Femme fatale, remember?"

Stifling an acerbic retort, he hopped out, and hustled around the front end of the Thunderbird, and pulled open the passenger door.

As she stepped out, the smokers took notice, watching her adjust her skirt, one of them gaping openly. Ignoring the attention, Crystal strode past them toward the entrance, her gait confident, her heels loud on the concrete. A guy with thick-rimmed glasses and a plaid shirt dived toward the door to pull it open for her, holding his vape pen behind his back.

As he got back behind the wheel, Slater had to grin. That had been quite an entrance.

Spotting an open meter a block away, Slater pulled in, and walked back to Alsace Acres. He nodded in greeting to the host, and didn't bother to look into the dining room, even though he wanted to. He had to let Crystal do her thing.

There were only a couple of people in the bar, at the far end, and he sat on a stool near the entrance. The TV facing the room was tuned to a baseball game, the volume down low.

The bartender, a portly guy in a bow tie and the familiar burgundy-vest uniform, stepped over. "What'll it be?"

"A small of the Kronenbourg," Slater said, and set a twenty on the bar top.

A minute later the guy set down a glass and whisked away the bill. Slater took a sip, knowing he was going to have to nurse it while Crystal worked, and looked at his phone.

Sometime later Crystal appeared, a vision in blue, drawing the bartender's lingering gaze. It wasn't necessarily about attraction, Slater knew, but about the gravity of her look. It demanded attention, like finding a Renaissance painting in a thrift store, or a rare orchid in a bamboo thicket.

Crystal stepped up to the bar just past his elbow, and didn't look at him, keeping her eyes on the TV screen.

"Let's go," she said quietly.

"I'll get the car," he said, not looking at her, just loud enough for her to hear. "Be out front in two minutes."

Before the bartender could step over, she was gone. Slater swirled his glass and slammed the last of his beer, then rose and walked out to the street.

Once he was in the Thunderbird, he circled the block and pulled up to the awning. Crystal stepped toward the curb, and waited, her little clutch in her upturned hand, like an unanswered question hanging in the air. He leaned down to glare at her, then figured it out. Jumping out, he ran around and opened the passenger door.

"You're going all-in on the femme fatale."

"Just drive." As he climbed in, she added, "There's a late-night diner a ways up. We can talk in there."

Slater pulled into the parking lot, and opened the door for her, and then the door to the diner. The place was crowded, and when they walked in, every eye was on Crystal, but she seemed oblivious.

The host subtly looked them over. "You can take the booth over there. The one in the window."

As they slid onto the benches, Slater said, "He wants you in the window. You're the best advertising they could hope for."

Crystal scoffed, and turned to the server as he stepped up. Clad in a white shirt with food stains on it, he was pushing sixty and balding. At least he kept his hair short. Straight guys didn't always get it, that the less you had the shorter it had to be.

"What can I get you?"

"A decaf," Crystal said.

"Same for me," Slater said, raising his voice, as the guy hadn't even glanced at him, fully fixated on Crystal.

Once he'd stepped away, Crystal said, "You need queer bait."

"What does that mean?"

"I talked to Woody. He's a friendly enough guy. I told him I was a fan of Danny and Frances. You said he'd mentioned replacing them, so I used that as my way in. I said, 'So are those animated fossils ever going to be updated with better music?'"

"Smart," Slater said. "I know he wants a bigger piece of that stage."

Crystal paused as the server set down two cups.

"He told me about a new club where he's working. He said the opening is tomorrow night."

"Greenleaf. I know about that place. If he's starting there tomorrow, why is he still working at Alsace?"

"I asked him that. He says he can do both, and swing it so the gigs don't overlap."

Holding her cup with both hands, she sipped delicately at it. She was trying not to mess up her lipstick, he realized.

"I suspect the band in a nightclub has to rehearse," Crystal said, "but the vocalist just has to bring their A-game. Woody said there's not much rehearsing in nightclubs compared to film work, so he can be on two stages without any trouble."

Slater sat back. "I knew there was a reason it had to be you."

"What are you talking about?"

"That's a really valuable insight. You thought it through, and you asked the right questions."

"It's just logic." She frowned. "What, you thought I was a simpleton?"

"I thought you might just take the compliment."

Slater threw up his hands. "So what's the thing about queer bait? Are you even allowed to say that word?"

"You find 'queer' offensive?"

"Not at all. I'm queer. It's just a little odd to hear it from the mouths of cis hetero folks."

"You don't know me," she said intently.

Slater waved a hand. "Moving on."

"So I flirted with him, full-on—I touched his arm, and picked a bit of lint off his lapel, and gazed into his eyes. Woody politely rebuffed me, and said he only dates men."

"Seriously?" Slater said. "I did not see that."

"Is your gaydar on the fritz? What made you think he was straight?"

"He drives a Bronco."

Her brow furrowed. "That's a really stupid assumption. I drive a Subaru—does that make me a lesbian?"

"If you butched your hair, and wore boots, it totally would."

"You're an idiot," she said firmly. "You drive a hoopty. What does that say about you?"

"It's a cool classic car, commensurate with my level of hotness."

Closing her eyes for a moment, she took a breath, then wrapped her hands around her cup. "I get the sense that Woody is on the level. He doesn't have that veneer that crooks have, and he's up front about his music, and the bands he's working with. My assessment is that he's a civilian."

"I want to say 'excellent work,' but I'm afraid

you'd take that as an insult."

"You owe me five dollars."

Slater shifted his hip to dig in his pants pocket. "Let me pay you now. I won't have to come to your office."

"Can you try to be a little subtle about it?" Crystal said. "Handing me all that cash is going to make me look like a prostitute."

"Nobody would ever mistake you for that." He peeled off the C-notes, and folded them, and tucked them under his saucer, then slid it toward her. "You look like a Westside philanthropist, or like you got lost on your way to one of those stupid awards shows."

A smirk played on her lips as she retrieved the bills, and stashed them in her little clutch, and snapped it closed. Slater rose with her and went to the register at the end of the counter, pulling out his cash. The clerk was a woman with sallow skin and smoker's wrinkles, her hair puffy and peroxided.

"You got your check, honey?" she said, her voice gravelly.

The guy who'd waited on them was loitering at the other end of the counter, arms folded. He called to her: "He was with the hot tomato. Table 9."

The clerk nodded and tapped at the register. "Here it is. Unleaded, times two. Try the pie next time."

Once he'd paid, he turned to find Crystal waiting by the entrance, a grin on her face.

"You love this," Slater said, as he opened the door for her. "Being the hot tomato. You're acting like you don't, but you do."

"I'll admit that a little bit of that kind of attention can be gratifying."

Slater opened the car door for her again, gently slamming it once she was inside.

"You're really down with the old-school gallantry," she said as he got behind the wheel. "It's almost like it comes naturally."

"I actually had a few lessons in it," Slater said, starting the engine. "When I was a teenager I got sent to a smarten-up camp in Wyoming."

"A finishing school for truculent urban hoodlums?"

"It was more like juvie with horses. There were no women there, but they taught us how to deal with them. If it's ever 1952 again, I've got the skills."

"Good manners never go out of style."

"It makes me glad I'm not straight. Those saps really have to work for it."

"And you don't have to work for it?"

"Not so much," Slater said, braking for a stoplight. "Like Woody. Now that I know he's gay, it won't take long to get into his pants."

"Wow." Crystal looked over at him. "For a guy who dresses like a day laborer, you've got quite the ego. What if he's with someone else? Or he's not attracted to you?"

"I don't think it'll be a problem. If I wear the right shirt, and lay down the right mack, he'll put out."

She sighed and looked out the side window. "You're a lot of man, Ibáñez."

When he pulled up at her front gate, Slater climbed out, and opened the car door, and held his hand for her. He watched as she grasped it and swung her legs out, knees locked together, using him to pull herself up.

"You should do more of this," he said. "You're good at it."

Crystal flashed a thin smile and shook her head. "I don't do field work."

Slater had to chuckle at that, and watched her open the little gate, and walk inside, her heels clacking on the concrete.

Back at his house, he waited for the garage door to roll down, then trudged up the stairs. It was that time of day: sex and then booze. But maybe he should be sated from all that time with Pike. They'd even had a quickie this morning. He could take a night off, he decided.

On the shelf in the kitchen cupboard the bourbon bottle sat next to Pike's decent scotch. He'd leave that for him, even though Pike didn't really drink, not the way Slater did. He found a tumbler and poured out his ration, then took a long pull from the bottle before he put it back. He'd been working all day—he deserved a little extra. He relished the heat of the liquid amber, the way the fumes burned in his nose.

He killed the lights and carried the tumbler over to the French doors, and propped them open, then stretched out on the sofa. Warm in his belly, the heady elixir was already slowing things down, damping the chaos. It felt weird now to be alone in this place. Pike was right, he thought, feeling his body sink into the sofa. You could totally hear the wind in the heavy fronds of the *washingtonias*.

TWELVE

BRIGHT DAYLIGHT STREAMED IN through the gauzy sheers when Slater woke. He'd forgotten to close the drapes again last night. He didn't remember coming down to bed, but his head didn't hurt, so he hadn't drunk much more than his ration.

Trudging upstairs, he started the coffee machine, then looked in the Frigidaire to find Miguel's foil chafing dish with the leftover rice and tortillas. Once he'd grabbed a fork, he carried the tray out onto the deck, walking past all the cut flowers. They were starting to look faded. He sat at the patio table to eat. The food was cold but he relished the warmth and the daylight, gradually waking up.

He poured himself a coffee, and took it back outside to savor it, then looked at his phone. In the tracking app he saw that Woody was on the road, driving east from his house. The green circle that estimated the Bronco's location snapped from place to place, and grew smaller and larger as the software reassessed the data it was reporting. As he watched, sipping his java, it finally stopped in Lincoln Heights, and the circle shrank. He zoomed in on the map. He knew that place—a giant thrift store, the mother of them all.

Slater knew how to navigate thrift stores, and this one was right over the hill, on the opposite side of that stupid stadium, so close he could almost hit it with a rock. If there was no ball game on, he could be there in a few minutes. If there was, it would take an hour. It would be faster just to go, he decided, rather than trying to figure it out online.

After he set the coffee cup in the sink, he trotted down to his bedroom and hurriedly got dressed, in yesterday's jeans and a tight black T-shirt. Down in the garage, he fired up the Thunderbird and backed into the street.

Traffic in the neighborhood was moving—as luck would have it, the stadium was dark. He drove hard on the way to the thrift store, roaring past the dawdlers, punching it through a yellow light, and in a few minutes he pulled into the fenced yard fronting the store. There were a lot of cars here, unsurprising given that it was Saturday morning, but he found a spot and hustled inside.

The thrift store had big open rooms like a warehouse, and Slater walked through the racks of clothes near the entrance, not looking at them but surveying the place and the people. There were a lot of bodies in here today. Had he missed his target? He reached for his phone, about to check the tracking app again for the Bronco, but then he spotted Woody, farther inside, among the furniture, his distinctive haircut catching his eye. Today he was wearing a brown-and-beige bowling shirt and tan trousers.

As he walked toward him, Slater assessed the space. There were several aisles among the jumble of chairs and tables and sofas. Woody was wandering in one of them, not moving very fast. Slater strode over and positioned himself farther up the aisle, in Woody's path, and then focused on the jumble of furniture in front of him—a haphazard stack of bed frames.

As Woody got closer, Slater saw in the periphery that he was about to walk behind him. Looking up, he caught his eye and spoke.

"Do you know anything about bed frames?"

Woody paused, his brow furrowing. "I don't work here."

Slater cracked a smile. "I figured. I meant as a consumer."

"Not really."

"What do you think of that one?" he said, and waved to a fuggly fabric-lined headboard.

"I don't mind the look of it. It's a good color."

"I guess." Slater folded his arms. "You can't really tie anything to it though."

Woody laughed, his tone rich and deep. "It sounds like you're a little kinky."

"Only if I'm with that kind of man." He waved

an arm. "It's not actually something I need for myself."

"It looks like there's more options behind it," Woody said, and took a few steps.

"So what are you looking for?" Slater said.

He turned back. "It was a shot in the dark. I need a music lectern, but they don't have any that I can see."

Greenleaf had a bunch of those on the bandstand, he remembered. "I didn't notice any either. Listen, do you have half a minute to grab a coffee?"

Woody hesitated. "I should get ready for work."

"You work the swing shift." Slater nodded. "Sweet."

"I work nights. Most people think that's sleazy."

"Well, I'm in insurance. It doesn't get any sleazier." Slater shrugged. "Nice try, but I win."

He laughed, his eyes bright. "What the hell. Do they have coffee here somewhere?"

"There's one right up the street. Go north, under the freeway. It's on the corner a few blocks up."

"Aren't you going to buy your bed frame?"

Slater glanced at it. "I'm going to need something much sleazier."

———•———

WHEN HE ROLLED PAST the coffee place, the yellow Bronco was already here, parked at a meter. He found a space farther up the block, then walked back, and stepped inside. Woody was at a table along the wall, and Slater nodded to him, then ordered his java, and carried the little cup over and sat across from him.

"Is that espresso?" Woody said.

Slater clicked his tongue. "A double."

"That sounds like rocket fuel. I guess it's early enough."

"So, I don't know what to do here."

Woody raised his eyebrows. "To drink coffee? It's just like drinking water. Hold it up to your mouth, and lean back, and tip the cup. Then you just kind of breathe in."

"I mean this." He waved a hand between them. "I don't know how to make small talk, and crack jokes like you just did, and sound intelligent. At the other end of it, though, I know that part."

"The other end? You mean the sex. You're saying you're good at sex."

"That's subjective," Slater said. "I'm saying that when I get my hands on a man, I know what I'm doing."

Woody watched him for a moment. "Do you have any idea how hot you are?"

He slowly shook his head. "There's nothing I can do about that. I can't really control it."

"Maybe we can cut to the chase."

"The main event?"

Woody laughed. "That's what I'm talking about."

"Excellent." Slater slammed his expresso. "My place is a couple minutes from here. I'll text you the address."

As Woody recited his number, Slater thumb-typed it into his phone. Once he'd sent him the details, he rose and headed out to the street.

A few minutes later, nosing into his garage, he killed the engine and caught sight of the yellow Bronco rolling up as the steel shutter descended. He stepped into the stairwell and opened the front door.

"Come on up," he said, and led Woody to his bedroom, stepping over to the window and yanking open the sheers to get more light.

"You already have a bed frame," Woody said.

"I need one for the other bedroom. I just moved in here."

Stepping closer, Woody grasped his arms, and massaged his shoulders. "Are you going to tie me up?"

"Do you want me to tie you up?"

"Not really. I want you to fuck me senseless."

"That, I can do." He met Woody's mouth, taut and warm, and reveled in it for a moment. Pulling away, he sat on the edge of the bed to untie his boots.

Watching him, Woody was breathing hard. He pulled off his shirt, then dropped his trousers. He had a great body, Slater saw, and he was already half hard.

Slater pulled his T-shirt off, and his jeans, and reached for Woody's hand, pulling him down onto the bed. Woody straddled him, and pressed his cock into Slater's junk. He leaned in, and they spent an intense minute with their mouths together. Massaging his cock, Slater mouthed his neck, running his other hand down his back.

Woody moved beside him, and grabbed his

cock, and squeezed. "You're ready."

Reaching for the bedside table, Slater scrabbled in a drawer and grabbed a condom.

"Let me." Woody took it, and ripped it open, and rolled it on him, then stroked him.

Slater grabbed the lube from the drawer and shifted next to Woody. Reaching between his legs, he massaged a thumb into him, starting slow. Woody leaned into it, and Slater moved closer, and soon penetrated him. Woody groaned with pleasure, and Slater built up to thrusting harder, making Woody yelp. Leaning in, with his nose in his hair, Slater strained into him as he climaxed.

After a moment he pulled back, and shifted down, and took him into his mouth. Woody was soon rock hard, and Slater worked him, one palm caressing his chest. His hand in Slater's hair, Woody arched his back as he came, his face contorted with the intensity.

Slater rolled onto his back and folded his arm over his eyes, catching his breath. As his heart rate slowed, he thought about Pike. Should he really be doing this, after Pike had used the *l* word? He'd even said it himself. Was this some kind of betrayal? The concept itself was mostly bullshit, he knew, part of a system designed to maintain the status quo, and he was doing this for work. But would Pike see it that way? They hadn't really talked about it. Maybe he was using that, the absence of any discussion, as an excuse to do whatever the hell he wanted.

Woody's voice pulled him from his thoughts. "This is a nice house. You said insurance is sleazy, but you must have a big job."

"I'd say I have a profitable job," Slater said. "What do you do for a living, working nights?"

"I'm a musician. A vocalist. There's all kind of vocalists, but my instrument is best suited to jazz music."

"Like torch songs and big band."

"Exactly." Woody reached for his hand and interlaced their fingers. "I work in nightclubs right now, and also in the entertainment industry sometimes, on film and TV soundtracks. I did a tequila commercial a while back. I worked on a cruise ship once. I'll never do that again."

"You make enough scratch to get by?"

"The entertainment industry and advertising pay pretty well. I'm lucky that my house is paid off. My parents left me some money. I just have to cover the taxes and the upkeep."

"There must be some rough characters in the nightclub business," Slater said. "Gangsters and greedy club owners."

"That's not really an issue for the musicians. The promoters have more problems. Getting an alcohol license is a pain in the ass, I've heard. I never saw any evidence of gangsters either. Somebody told me the feds worked hard in the old days to keep them out of LA's entertainment industry."

"So you personally don't have any enemies in that world."

"Not that I know of."

"Do you sleep with women too?"

Woody eyed him, his brow furrowed. "Not

since I figured out I like men better."

"So there's no jealous women out there looking for you."

"Why would you ask me that?"

"I'm curious about what your life is like. It's not every day I meet a show-biz canary."

"I'm really more of a nightclub canary," Woody said. "And while we're expressing our curiosity, I'm curious as to where I can find a towel."

"The bathroom is right there." Slater sat up. "I'll bring you one."

Slater took a minute to wash his junk, and grabbed a towel, and walked back to the bed. Woody had shifted up, sitting propped on the pillows.

"Who's Reddy Kilowatt?" Woody said.

"Why are you asking?"

"It came up on your screen. A text from Reddy Kilowatt. It said, 'I can still smell you on my shirt. I don't want to change.'"

Slater tossed the towel on his belly and scooped up his phone from the bedside table. "Why are you looking at my phone?"

"It buzzed."

Sitting on the edge of the bed, Slater texted Pike a quick response:

> Imagine my arms wrapped around you right now, my hot breath on your neck, my rock-hard manhood inside you.

After he pressed SEND, he looked at Woody, and gestured with the phone. "He's a guy I'm kind of getting sticky with."

"So why are you sleeping with me?"

"It's not at that stage yet. Where we're exclusive."

"That message makes it sound like he's into you."

"I didn't want to mislead you," Slater said.

"I'm not husband-shopping here." He reached for Slater's arm and pulled him closer. "I just wanted to have some fun with a fellow thrift-store shopper."

Stretching out beside him, Slater caressed his chest. "That actually rings true."

Woody chuckled. "I'm flattered that you believe me. Is his name really Reddy Kilowatt?"

"It's a nickname. The first time we met, he tased me."

"I guess that's one way to get a man's attention. What does he call you?"

"I don't know if I should be talking about him with you."

"Unless you're going to buy me jewelry," Woody said, "I promise I won't get jealous."

"He calls me the forty-niner."

"Are you his forty-ninth hookup or something?"

"He says I'm narrow-minded about pants," Slater said. "I made fun of his stretchy trousers. I only wear classic jeans, like during the gold rush in the Sierra. Not stretchy chinos or denim-colored spandex."

"I get it. You're like a miner forty-niner." Woody squeezed his fingers. "What's this guy like?"

"Well, I'm not even sure what he looks like. It's like staring into the sun."

"That sounds a little extreme."

"He's the sunrise, and the sunset, and all the daylight in between. And after that he's all the stars and all the moonlight."

"Oh, man." Woody laughed. "You're obsessed."

"I've been wondering about that. I do think I still have some objectivity about him. Like I can see he wears stupid clothes, and he's all calm and glib sometimes when the situation calls for outrage and fury."

"So he's not perfect."

"Far from it."

"That's actually a good thing," Woody said. "You don't want to put him on a pedestal. He won't live up to your expectations."

"The part that I can't think clearly about is the connection we have. It's like there's park, and there's fifth gear." He mimed manipulating a gear shift with his hand. "And there's nothing in between."

"No nuances, no half measures."

"Is that messed up?" Slater said. "It's kind of new territory for me."

"The best dating advice I ever got was to just be yourself. This guy will either be able to handle it or he won't."

"I suspect that's excellent advice."

"I'm crushed out on a guy right now too," Woody said.

"Is he hot?"

"Smoking hot. I guess I should say white hot. He's a little white twink."

"Twinks are fun," Slater said. "You have to be

careful though. Some of them can be delicate. Like stemware."

"I have no idea how to connect with him."

"Just be yourself."

Woody chuckled. "He walks into the room and I'm so nervous."

"Seriously? You seem so comfortable in your skin." Slater thought of the presence Woody commanded at Alsace Acres, the confidence he projected.

"It's because I'm too into him. He's the drummer at the club I'm starting at tonight."

"Is it true that drummers are nuts?"

"I wouldn't say that. Maybe they're idiosyncratic. Lars seems a little OCD. I watched him organizing his keys on his key ring. My god, like it matters what order they're in. But I wouldn't say there's a drummer type."

"That's a great name," Slater said. "Lars."

"So Midwest, right? I thought he might be a meth head, but he's not. He's just upbeat like that naturally."

"Tweakers take way too much energy."

"I'd rather do a tweaker than a purple-drank guy. They pass out in the middle of the sex." He waved a hand. "Purple drank is codeine syrup."

"I know what purple drank is." Slater eyed him sidelong. "I usually hear it called GI gin."

"That's because you're white."

"All the shrinks I got sent to in my youth would call that labeling," Slater said. "And white folks don't actually consider me white."

"You know what I mean." Reaching for Slater's phone, he glanced at the screen. "I should go. I have to work."

Slater watched as he started to get dressed. "The new nightclub?"

"It's called Greenleaf. Upstairs at Sackett's."

"That's a fun place. A hundred years ago I used to eat there with my parents on Saturday afternoon."

"The bar is really beautiful," Woody said, buttoning his shirt. "You should come tonight. I'm working so I won't be able to hang out. I know the music will be good. It's not really a cabaret, but there's a floor show."

"What kind of acts?"

"Classy stuff. A ventriloquist, a woman who juggles things, these skinny acrobat guys. There might be stand-up."

"Is there a dress code?"

Woody was gazing at his phone, and answered absently. "Sort of. You should wear a sports jacket or a suit." He leaned in to kiss him. "That was fun."

Listening to his footfalls on the stairs, then the front door closing, Slater closed his eyes, feeling warm and sated. He knew he should get up and be productive, but it was just too comfortable here. He couldn't help but drift off.

THIRTEEN

WHEN SLATER WOKE, HE pulled on a pair of boxers and a T-shirt, then went upstairs to eat more of Miguel's leftovers, sitting at the table outside. It was in the shade now, but it was still plenty warm out. He checked the tracking app on his phone.

Woody wasn't at Greenleaf—the Bronco was way over on the Westside, on Abbot Kinney. Zooming in on the location, he switched to the street view. It was parked in front of a shop with a big green sign that said LIMEADE. Was that some new trend? He knew limes were expensive. Ordinary *taqueros* had long ago replaced them with lemons as a garnish. No surprise someone was selling them on the Westside as an exclusive lifestyle experience. But it seemed unlikely that the guy would drive across town just for that.

Panning around the image, he saw there was a

lot of retail on that stretch—clothing stores, a hair salon, restaurants. The building Woody was parked in front of had an upper floor with windows facing the street. Commercial, it looked like, not residential. At the end of the building, past the shop, was a heavy door. There was no name on it, but it had a street number posted above. That had to lead to the offices upstairs.

Thinking about it, that was a busy boulevard. Maybe Woody just happened to park there. He could have gone to any of a dozen businesses nearby. Slater did a search for the street number, and soon found the name of the tenant in the upstairs office: a business called Novo Paradigm. Its website was flashy, with panning photos of a stylish office interior, and text that explained Novo Paradigm offered "modern fiscal solutions." But there was no further detail about what that meant. Without any context it sounded extremely shady—loan-sharking, maybe, or money laundering, or tax evasion.

Digging through the search results for the company, he got the sense that it was built around one person, a man named Hezekiah Davenport. Had his mother named him that, or was it an affectation? A photo showed Hezekiah to be a thin guy in his mid-thirties with mousy brown hair, a nineteenth-century mustache, and little round glasses. In another photo he was wearing a monocle.

In every image that came up he was dressed in yellow and dark red—the jacket and the shirt, or the shirt and the neck scarf. Sometimes the shirt was red and the jacket was mustard yellow. Each time it was different garments but always that color combination. In one photo he wore a yellow shirt and a red plaid vest. Those were loud colors. It seemed like a weird signature style.

Slater ran a search for "Woody Newkirk" with "Novo Paradigm," and the lone useful result that came up, from a website that sold stock media photos, was a shot of Hezekiah with Woody, the pair of them arm in arm, beaming at the camera. Hezekiah was in red plaid again, and Woody was wearing a tux. They stood in front of a wall with a repeating logo pattern on it. Other photos in the series showed different people standing at the same background—it was some D-list awards event. Unlike any of the other photos Slater had seen, in this one Hezekiah was smiling so broadly that his teeth showed. They were uneven, almost snaggled. That meant he'd either grown up working-class or had grown up abroad.

Slater stared at the photo. "Modern fiscal solutions." It made this guy sound like a damn crook. What was his connection to Woody?

He checked the tracker again and saw that the Bronco was on the move now, headed east on the 10. It hadn't been parked at Novo Paradigm for very long, but long enough to take a meeting. No way had he driven there to buy overpriced lime juice. That red-carpet photo implied that Woody knew Hezekiah Davenport. He'd been at the guy's office.

Slater needed to look into this knucklehead, but he hated driving to the Westside. There was always so much traffic, especially at this time of day. But it was going to hurt no matter when he did it.

Down in the garage, he waited for the door to roll up and then backed into the street. It took a while to get to Venice, and eventually he was crawling along Abbot Kinney in the congested traffic. There were even more restaurants and high-end shops here these days, but the familiar chains were starting to creep in, the footwear and fast-fashion brands. That was predictable—corporate America was going to turn this into another soulless retail strip and suck it dry. While that was happening the trendoids who'd pioneered it would move on.

There was an open meter just past the building, and Slater pulled in, and walked the length of the limeade store toward the entrance to the office. The shop was styled in lime green, the counters and the signage and the white-and-green checkered floor tiles. The line of people waiting for limeade stretched from the counter out to the sidewalk.

"Idiots," Slater muttered, glancing inside.

The door at the end of the building had a small corporate logo on it now, and the words NOVO PARADIGM. That hadn't been there in the street view— Hezekiah hadn't been here very long. When Slater tried the handle, the door was unlocked, and he stepped inside and trotted up the stairs.

The front office was the room he'd seen in the website images, paved in pale blue carpet, topped by sleek white chairs and cabinets, a glass desk in the middle. Three abstract canvases hung on the wall opposite the windows onto the street. The marketing boilerplate on the website mentioned "chic modernity," and this space was definitely intended to create that impression.

There were no security cameras here, and there hadn't been any in the stairwell or at the front door. Either Hezekiah was broke, or naive, or up to something that he didn't want recorded.

At the side, beyond the artworks, a hallway led farther back, but up front a woman was parked behind the glass desk. Her hair was messy, and blond, and cut below her ears. It was hard to tell whether it was just utilitarian or a trendy-casual look calculated to complement the decor. She looked up as Slater entered, eyeing him with wide-set blue eyes. Why was everyone in this neighborhood white and Anglo?

She gave him the once-over and said, "*¿Entrega?*"

"Why do you assume I speak Spanish?" Slater said.

"Deliveries are from the alley. It's called Alhambra Court." She whirled a finger in the air. "Just go around back. You'll see the same building number painted over the service door."

"I'm not the help, toots," Slater snapped. "You can check the patronizing bullshit."

She frowned. "What do you want?"

"I need to talk to Hezekiah Davenport."

"Il Capitano."

He threw up a hand. "What does that mean?"

"That's his name. Hezekiah Davenport is his legal name, but no one calls him that."

"OK, then I need to talk to Il Capitano."

"He's not here," she said. "Can I ask what this is regarding?"

"When will he be back?"

"I can't give out that information."

Slater clenched his teeth, and pulled a business card out of his hip pocket, and stepped closer to set it on her desk. "Tell him he needs to call me."

"Il Capitano is a busy man," she said, not looking at it. "He doesn't take sales calls."

"I'm not selling," he said, raising his voice. "I'm running an insurance investigation. If he doesn't call me, I'll subpoena him, and he'll have to talk to the lawyers. That'll be in front of a video camera, in a day-long deposition, in a crummy windowless office downtown."

She frowned. "He's been named in a legal proceeding?"

"Not yet, but if I don't get some answers, he will be. The choice is simple. Il Capitano can talk to me for ten minutes, or I can escalate, and if that happens"—he jabbed a finger at her—"that's on you."

Walking out, he smiled to himself as he trotted down the stairs. If they were seasoned lowlifes, she wouldn't buy it, but if he'd managed to plant even a seed of doubt, the guy's fear or curiosity would get the better of him, and he'd call. Hopefully it would pan out, as this trip had a sharp cost in terms of his time—it was going to take him an hour to get back downtown.

Once he was at his house, up in his bedroom, Slater opened his closet and pulled out his tux. It was midnight blue and cut tight to flatter his body. It would work without a necktie, he decided, and pulled on a white shirt, leaving the collar open. Stepping into the pants, he was glad to find they still fit.

Pulling on the jacket, he stepped over to the floor mirror and looked himself over. Pike was right: he actually needed a floor mirror. They'd seen it when they'd gone to the furniture store. Pike said the bathroom mirrors weren't enough. Slater never would have thought of it, but here was the proof, he was actually using the damn thing.

His phone buzzed, and he grabbed his jeans from the floor and fished it out. Area code 718. Was that New York? He answered, "Ibáñez."

"Violet told me you wanted to talk to me," a man's voice said. "Something about an insurance claim."

Slater knew exactly who it was, but he said, "Who is this?"

"Il Capitano. At Novo Paradigm. I just got back to the office."

"I am not driving out to the middle of nowhere again today," Slater said. "That ship has sailed."

"Venice isn't the middle of nowhere. It's a cultural crucible. It's actually the middle of everything."

He scoffed. "Keep telling yourself that. When can you meet me that's not today?"

"I'll be in the office tomorrow."

"A man who works on Sunday. You must be

conducting some serious business. I'll be there in the early afternoon."

Not waiting for a response, he ended the call.

The tux was as much of a concession to formality as he was going to make, he decided. No way was he going to wear the dress shoes. They had such thin soles it was like walking around in sock feet, like he could feel every crack in the sidewalk. He pulled on his boots and tucked his pant legs into them.

When he drove up to the parking structure on Seventh, across from Sackett's, he saw there was a plastic folding barricade blocking the ramp. When he got closer, he could read the sign on it: FULL. Cruising around the corner, he found another structure a few blocks away, and walked back to Sackett's.

The restaurant was open, and surprisingly busy. There was probably a dedicated entrance to Greenleaf, with an elevator, but he knew how to get there through the dining room. He walked through the forest decor, and went up the stairs to the overflow dining space. Even down here he could hear the band, playing an upbeat jazz number, with the unmistakable depth and richness of live music. The stairwell leading up didn't have the chain across it tonight.

Parked on a stool at the top of the stairs was a muscle-bound bouncer, dressed in black, his head shaved. He gave Slater a disinterested once-over as he walked in. No one was here to charge cover, he realized. Maybe that would change once the place had been open a while.

The music filled the room, and he eyed the band

on the bandstand. There was no sign of Woody. Three straight couples were dancing out front, swing-style, an energetic and eye-catching display. They were dressed for dancing, the women in billowy skirts and the men in baggy trousers. It was too picture-perfect for them to be customers who were incidentally dressed that way and knew how to do it—Les James must have hired them.

Most of the tables around the room were occupied, with black-vested waitstaff floating around. A few people were standing at the edge of the dance floor. Overall it seemed like a good turnout for an opening night.

Slater looked over the band. The musicians were wearing dark-green velour jackets, and there were more of them than at Alsace Acres. Besides a guitar and a keyboard, there was a lot of brass—a trumpet, a trombone, and a couple of saxes. On the left the drum kit had GREENLEAF emblazoned on the front of the bass. The drummer looked to be in his twenties, his dark red hair slicked back. That had to be Lars. His expression was intent as he manipulated his sticks with manic fervor.

Walking over to the bar, Slater leaned in and ordered a Corona. Once he had it in hand, he stood at the side of the dance floor and watched the band. The dancers vacated the space at the end of the song, and when the next song ended, after a round of applause, a woman stepped out on stage, wearing a chic red dress, her hair styled to tumble on her shoulders. It wasn't until she spoke that he realized it was Les James.

"Give it up for the band," she said, and clapped, looking back at them. The crowd obediently applauded with her. "A little later we'll get to the floor show. We have some great acts for you tonight. But before that, it gives me great pleasure to introduce our vocalist, the inimitable Woody Newkirk."

To more applause, Woody stepped onto the stage as Les strode off. He was wearing the same green velour jacket as the band. With a broad smile, he stood at the front, exuding confidence, one hand resting casually on the mike stand. The band started up, and soon came Woody's deep rich voice: "My baby don't care for shows / My baby don't care for clothes / My baby just cares for me."

His voice was powerful, Slater thought, watching him. He didn't even need amplification. It had to take a lot of work to sound that smooth and consistent, and Woody made it look effortless. He was a born entertainer. Crystal thought he was a civilian, and talking to him today, he'd seemed guileless. But if he could so easily summon this polished professional persona, maybe the regular-guy routine had been a snow job too.

It was hard to tell whether he'd noticed Slater, even though their eyes met, as he was making eyes at everyone in the room. Probably not, he decided. There was a spotlight in his face. He likely couldn't see anything.

Woody did two more songs, then made a little bow and flourish, and he and the band left the stage. Slater wandered over toward the hallway on the side where the band had exited, and paused near the end of the bar. He couldn't really go into the back. The door was clearly marked STAFF ONLY.

As he sipped at his Corona, surveying the space, the drummer strode out that door and into the main room. Lars. He was still wearing his band jacket. As he walked by, sensing Slater's gaze, he glanced at him and flashed a smile. The guy had that idiosyncratic paleness that redheads had, but he wouldn't call him excessively foxy. More interesting was the small pin on his lapel: a dark blue circle with a triangle in the tmiddle. Lars went over to a table and stood talking to its occupants. They seemed to know him.

A few minutes later Woody walked out of the back, without his band jacket, subtle sweat stains visible in the armpits of his white shirt. He spotted Slater, and stepped over, and squeezed his arm.

"I'm so glad you made it," he said. "I love that suit."

"I wish I could say the same about your band outfit."

"It's a great color, though, isn't it? It goes with the blue around the stage."

"It doesn't fit very well," Slater said. "No one can see your amazing body."

Woody chuckled. "Maybe it's better that people focus on my musical chops."

"Your voice is totally seductive. Everyone in the place was in your thrall."

"Thank you," he said, and made a little bow from the neck.

"Why isn't there a band leader?"

"Sally's in charge," Woody said. "She's first sax. Maybe you can't see it from out here, but she sets the time."

"She's the one on the left?"

"The Asian one. She's not really physically imposing, but she has strong opinions. Sally and Les argue about the music at every opportunity. Les wants us to be sweet, with the sentimental songs, and Sally wants it to be hard, so people will dance."

"Do you get to sing more when it's sweet?"

"It's about the same. The hard songs are more work for me though."

"I saw Lars," Slater said.

Woody cracked a smile. "Doesn't he just send you?"

"You didn't tell me he was a redhead."

"He's so hot, right?"

"Totally hot," Slater said. "Redheads are like blonds with an upgrade."

"Did you see the way his trousers fit?"

"I didn't. Is he stacked?"

"Oh, yeah."

"Listen, I have intel on him."

Woody's eyebrows shot up. "Like what?"

"Have you ever had any dealings with twelve-step, or twelve-steppers?"

"You mean AA? Not really."

"There's all kinds of programs. Alcoholics, narcotics, sexual compulsives. Even freaking codependents."

"You think Lars is a twelve-stepper?"

"He's wearing a twelve-step pin on his band

jacket," Slater said. "That means it's important to him. Either he's in recovery, or somebody he cares about is."

"Interesting," Woody said, "but so what?"

"So turn it into something actionable. Point to the pin and say 'One day at a time' or 'Keep coming back.'"

"Those are twelve-step slogans? Doesn't that violate the anonymous part?"

"It's only anonymous if you want it to be. I'm betting he'll want to make the connection with you. He'll ask you why you recognize the symbol."

"I can't really say I'm in twelve-step."

"You can say someone you love is in program. A friend or a relative. It gives you an excuse for not knowing too much about it."

"And I don't have to name the person, because it's supposed to be anonymous." Woody threw up his hands. "Thank you—this is potentially huge."

"If it doesn't work," Slater said, "do you want a plan B?"

Woody chuckled. "Hit me."

"Lars looks a little simpleminded."

"Rude," he said, and frowned. "How could you possibly know that?"

"I downloaded his high school transcripts. I never saw so many D-minuses on one page."

"You did not."

"It's just a guess," Slater said. "But with dumb guys, you have to talk about something dumb."

"I so hope he's not dumb."

"What difference does it make? You can still

fuck him." Slater waved a hand. "You have to talk about food or celebrities. Ask him if he heard about Artémise."

"What happened to her?"

"There's always something, isn't there? Her man cheated on her, or she had a temper tantrum at a photo shoot, or her private jet blew a tire when she was landing at Tulum. If he's into her, he'll know."

"Celebrities or food," Woody said. "Got it."

"With food, keep it simple. Ask him if he likes mayonnaise."

"You have got to be kidding."

"It's just a starting point. It can't get any dumber, so most likely the road will be upward from there."

"I'm going to call you the twink whisperer."

"It's not an esoteric skill," Slater said, "but I do know how to get into guys' pants."

"Hopefully we can connect over twelve-step. I just hope he's not a junkie."

"He's wearing the pin. That means he's working the steps."

"It doesn't mean he's not a junkie."

"Twelve-steppers are great," Slater said. "I work with one. If they're doing it right, they're easy to be around. They don't put demands on you. They make excellent boyfriend material."

FOURTEEN

A WOMAN STEPPED OUT OF the door to the back, wearing the band uniform. Slight and half a head shorter than Woody, she had her black hair tied back. Sally, he'd called her. The band leader. She walked up to them, and nodded to Slater, and spoke to Woody.

"That was tight."

"I'm glad you thought so," Woody said. "Your second got a little frisky."

"Don't worry. I'll handle him."

Shop talk, Slater realized, and stepped away, toward the bar. He leaned on it and waved the bartender over. Once he had another Corona in hand, he turned back to look over the room.

A man was standing with Woody and Sally now, dressed in a sports jacket. A customer, Slater decided, not one of the band. He had broad shoulders but he couldn't really assess the guy's butt under his jacket. His body language said he was intoxicated, and Slater couldn't hear what he said, but Sally's expression suddenly shifted, and he could hear her clearly: "You racist fuck."

The guy shoved her shoulder, even though he was a lot bigger than her, and Sally took a step back. Where was security, Slater wondered, glancing around. He took a swig of his beer, and set the bottle on the bar, and strode over to them.

The drunk was shouting now, gesturing toward Sally. Slater grabbed his shoulder, and spun him around, and slapped his face, right and then left, a firm kovac.

"Knock it off," Slater said through his teeth.

Younger than he expected, the guy looked to be college age. His eyes were glassy, his face contorted with surprise. This was going to be easy.

"Mexican," the guy growled, his fists balled. Almost as an afterthought, he added, "thug," and jutted his chin.

"The thug is you," Slater said, pointing a finger at him. "You. You're the thug."

As he'd anticipated, he lunged at Slater, and Slater quickly crouched, and went for his legs. It was part of a wrestling move, something he'd learned in middle school, but he didn't grapple with the guy, instead just pushing under him, and then stood erect. The guy toppled to the floor, flat on his belly.

"Why do you make me do this to you?" Slater shouted, and kicked him in the ribs. "Why do you make me hurt you?"

He groaned and tried to roll onto his side.

Slater forced himself to step back.

"Stay down," he demanded.

The drunk started to get to his hands and knees. Slater was about to kick him again when a security guard stepped up. It was the thick guy who'd been on the door, bald and dressed in black. He pulled the drunk to his feet with one arm. The guy seemed dazed now, the fight gone out of him, and the guard frog-marched him toward the stairs.

Another beefy guy dressed in black stepped up to Slater.

"You too, *cholo*," he said. "Let's go. Do not make me take you down."

Before Slater could react, Woody stepped between them.

"The drunk was the problem," he said to the guard. "Slater did your job, and slowed him down. Where were you?"

"When there's a fistfight, everybody involved gets eighty-sixed. That's the rules."

"If he goes, I go," Woody said. "Maybe you should check with Les first whether she's willing to lose her vocalist."

The guard looked Slater over. "How tight are you?"

Adjusting his jacket, Slater spoke through his teeth. "I am not a *cholo*."

He hesitated, studying his face. "I guess you're OK," he said finally, and walked away.

Slater clapped Woody on the shoulder, by way of thanking him, and eyed Sally. Her face was contorted in disgust.

"You're welcome," Slater said.

Sally scoffed, and shook her head, and walked toward the door into the back.

"What was that about?" Woody demanded, scowling at him.

"He was going to flatten her," Slater said, and waved an arm toward Sally. "Why is she pissed at me?"

"She was handling it herself. Why did you have to get aggressive?"

"He was escalating. Could you not see that? I suppose I could have called an arbitrator, or a mindfulness coach, or a healing-crystal vendor, but I don't have one in my contact list."

Woody sighed. "I've got to go back to work," he said, and walked away.

Walking back to the bar, Slater found his beer, and stood near the dance floor, and took a long pull from the bottle. What the hell was wrong with people? He'd deftly taken out a threatening drunk, yet somehow in this equation Slater was the asshole.

A few minutes later the band walked on, and got comfortable, and played another set. They sounded great. Woody sang again. The guy was so talented. Listening to him was easy, and almost made up for him being a dick about the drunk.

Les walked out from the back and strolled past the bar, her red dress drawing Slater's eye. As she glanced at him, she did a double take.

"Were you in here yesterday?" she said, leaning close and raising her voice to be heard over the music.

"You certainly clean up nicely," Slater said. "You said tonight was your opening. You managed to pull in a crowd."

Les smiled and touched his arm. "It's a good start. Nice to see you. Have fun."

She stepped away, approaching a table of her customers. He should probably leave, he knew. If Woody found out he'd been in here before, he'd have questions.

He guzzled his beer but lingered, enjoying the music and Woody's rich voice. They did a few more numbers, and eventually the band trooped off the stage, replaced by Les, who stood in the spotlight for a moment, faux clapping and beaming, showing her perfect teeth. When the applause died down, Les spoke.

"Magic is all around us, and tonight we have some magic for you. In just a moment we'll start the floor show."

Woody walked out of the back and approached him. Sweat glistened on his forehead.

"I saw you talking to Les," he said.

"The host? She seems nice enough. She told me to drink more, and call some friends."

His brow furrowed. "It seemed like she recognized you."

"Maybe she thought I was someone important," Slater said. "It's the suit. I don't think she saw me taking out the trash. If she had, she would have thanked me."

"OK," he said, but he didn't look convinced.

"Listen, I have to go."

"What about the floor show? It's starting right now."

"I've already seen you sing. That was the best part. Go lock it down with Lars."

Woody grinned and squeezed his arm, then walked toward the door into the back.

A chubby guy in a black tux stepped onto the stage, holding a big doll with buggy eyes. As the lights went up, he took a little bow, in unison with the doll. Slater walked toward the top of the stairs, half watching the stage.

"Thank you," the performer said. "I'm the Amazing Snorri, and this is Carl."

The doll swiveled its head, surveying the room, and blinked. "What are you chumps gawking at? It looks like a discount store exploded in here."

Near the top of the staircase Slater stopped to watch for a minute. He'd never seen that before— an insult ventriloquist.

Snorri held out a hand, and with a flourish and a snap a fuchsia-colored flower appeared in it. The crowd responded with wan applause.

The doll said, "That's it? You philistines. Didn't you pick up on the 'amazing' part?"

A few people laughed, and there was a round of slightly more enthusiastic applause. A woman had paused next to Slater, watching the performance. She had short hair, and a print dress, her arms folded.

"He's mixing his genres," she said. "Ventriloquism and stand-up."

"With a little magic thrown in," Slater said.

"Maybe it works for people with a short attention span."

He eyed her sidelong. "You and I are both watching."

She chuckled at that.

Over by the STAFF ONLY door, Slater caught sight of Woody, standing in the shadows. Lars was with him, his back to the wall. Ignoring the floor show, Slater watched them for a moment. More than casual chitchat, the pair of them were immersed in an intent conversation. Had they connected over twelve-step, he wondered, or Artémise, or mayonnaise?

Mumbling "Good night" to the woman next to him, he turned and headed down the stairs, and walked to where he'd parked the Thunderbird, and drove to his house.

Upstairs he ditched the tux and pulled on a T-shirt and boxers, then went up to the kitchen and poured his ration into a tumbler, resentful at the paucity. With Pike not around, he didn't really have to behave, he decided, and poured another couple of fingers. Eyeing the vases with the fading flowers lining the room, he killed the lights, and turned on the radio, and stretched out on the sofa. He sipped the heady golden liquid, relishing the burn.

Sometime later he woke to his phone buzzing, and felt for it on the floor, next to the empty tumbler. Pike, he saw, and picked up.

"Hey, forty-niner. Did I wake you?"

"No," Slater managed, his tongue thick. "What's going on?"

"I was just thinking about you. I wanted to hear your voice."

"I get it," Slater said. "I miss you. I miss the way your skin feels, and the way your hair smells."

"Back at you."

"What did you do today?"

As Pike spoke, he half listened, and half dozed, occasionally murmuring acknowledgment. Just hearing his voice was intoxicating. Better than anything on the radio. Better even than bourbon.

FIFTEEN

S LATER'S HEAD WAS THROBBING when he woke, and he winced at the daylight. He was in his own bed. Sitting up, he took a deep breath. He'd overdone it. The room smelled of the cloying sweet tang of digested booze seeping out of his pores.

"Idiot," he muttered, and grabbed his phone to check his calls and texts. He hadn't drunk-dialed anyone. That was a relief. Maybe it wouldn't be too bad. He wasn't nauseous, and the room wasn't spinning. After a few deep breaths, he forced himself to stand up, and went to pee, and then went up to the kitchen.

The last of Miguel's tortillas felt a little stiff, he decided, pulling the foil tray of leftovers out of the icebox, and he threw them out. He ate some of the rice with the salsa, and the beans were still good. Once he'd had half a cup of coffee, his head felt better, and he called Chila.

"I was wondering when I was going to hear from you," she said as she picked up. "What have you got for me?"

"Can I come by your office?"

"I'm not there today," Chila said quickly. "I'll come to you. Are you in your office?"

"Meet me there in an hour," he said, and ended the call.

She must have forgotten that it was Sunday. Nobody would be in the office. But when you were unemployed, one day started to look like the next. No surprise that she lost track.

Downstairs, Slater tried to shower off the stink of last night's bender, then got dressed, in a tan linen shirt Doris had bought for him. She said the fabric was cooler in the heat, and it was supposed to get hot today. Tucking it into his jeans, he hustled down to his garage and drove to the Fashion District.

No Max and no Etta, he found, stepping into his office. Etta still went to mass at her degenerate church every week, for some reason, and Sunday was Max's girlfriend's day off. He clicked his tongue to greet the statue of Rey Pascual, placidly watching the front door, then stuck his head into Max's office to make absolutely sure he was alone.

Once he was comfortable at his own desk, he checked the time. Chila was late. Twenty minutes was the limit for LA flakiness—less than that counted as on time, and more than that was late. Unlocking his computer, he waited a while longer, and half-heartedly worked on an expense report for O'Dowd, their accountant. The task was basically formulating numerical fiction, and the pain it caused in his brain compounded his hangover. How fucking stupid was that, getting so soused that he could barely focus today.

Checking the time again, he dialed Chila's number and got her voice mail.

"You'd better be dead," Slater told the machine, "because if you just stood me up, I'll make you wish you were."

He set the phone down, and a moment later it buzzed with a text:

Chill out. I got held up. I'm on my way.

Eventually he heard a knock at the front door, and got up to pull it open. Chila had her hair tied back and wore jeans and a stretchy athletic top. She looked sweaty. This building was cool enough inside, but he knew it was hot out.

"Finally," he said.

Chila scowled at him. "What is wrong with you?"

"What are you talking about?"

"You just threatened me on voice mail for being a few minutes late."

"Forty minutes late. I have a low tolerance for being disrespected."

"Are you going to let me in?" she demanded.

Slater stepped back, and extended his arm, closing the door behind her. In his office, she sat across from him, and he rolled his chair closer to his desk.

"Would madam like a biscotti, or an espresso with a lemon twist? Perhaps a moist towelette after her difficult journey?"

"Snap out of it," she demanded. "I am not acting entitled."

"Except with my time. You know, people tell me on a regular basis that I'm the asshole." He spread his palms. "Sometimes I know it's true, and sometimes I'm not quite sure. This one seems pretty cut and dried. It's you."

Chila waved impatiently. "So what's the status of your inquiries?"

"I'm very close to finding the guy," Slater said, leaning back. "Can you give me the paperwork on his payout? I can present it to him when I locate him."

"No way." She shook her head. "I need to meet Woodrow myself. What do you mean you're close?"

"I'm working a couple of leads."

"Is he in town?"

Slater laced his fingers behind his head. "Might be."

Anger flashed in her eyes, and she stood up, and slapped her palm on the desktop. "You'd better not be holding out on me, you cheap hood. I'm the one who's paying you."

Slater sat up. "You'd better not take a poke at me. You really don't want me to punch back."

Red-faced, her lip curled into a sneer, and she dropped back into the chair.

"Why do you need to meet him yourself?" Slater said.

"Because I say so. What are the leads you're working on?"

"I can't really lay it all out. It's insider stuff."

Chila scoffed and rose. "What a fricking waste of my morning."

"Don't be that way," Slater said, and got up. "It's just business. You can't tell me why you need to meet him in person, and I'm not going to reveal my sources. It doesn't really change anything."

"Then find him," she said intently.

Slater stepped around his desk. "I'll walk out with you. I know you're afraid of the blue-collar types around here."

"I'm not afraid of anybody. Especially not you."

"Where did you park?"

"In the lot across the street."

"Me too."

They rode the elevator down and crossed to the parking lot, and Chila paused at a dark-green Camry. Its lights flashed as she pressed her key fob to unlock it.

She jutted her chin at him. "You'd better not be fucking with me."

"I'm working for you, Chila, and only you. Day and night."

She scoffed and climbed into her car.

Walking over to the Thunderbird, he repeated her plate number in his head until he got behind the wheel and typed it into a note on his phone. He waited until she pulled out of the lot, then drove to Andy's.

When Andy opened his door, he frowned at

him. "You owe me money."

Slater followed him inside. Andy always kept the place cold, to compensate for his high-revving metabolism, and it felt especially good today, coming in from the heat and with the toxic by-products of cheap bourbon still making his muscles ache.

"You know I'm good for it," Slater said. "And you'd better not try to chisel me just because you're pissed at me."

Andy dropped into his desk chair and looked him over. "Rough night?"

"Do I look that bad?"

"No worse than usual. Like you got run over by … a truck." He waved dismissively. "I liked your … friend Pike."

"He's back in Albuquerque."

"I get why you're into him. He's … confident, and intuitive."

"I can't really do much about it," Slater said. "It seems to be some kind of chemical process."

He raised his voice. "Why are you here?"

"Can you find a home address for the woman you researched for me? Isidra Suárez."

"I think I already got that. It would have been … on her unemployment claim. Let me check." He swiveled to his desk, and pulled on his gauntlets, and peered at the screen. "She lives in Montebello," he said finally. "I'll text it … to you."

"Since you already had it," Slater said, "I'm sure there's no extra charge."

Andy swiveled toward him. "You're on … thin ice with me, Ibáñez."

"What's between us doesn't have to change. I want you. I've always wanted you. You know that."

"Just not as much as you want … the brunette. But I believe you. Only it's never been … about me. You've never been … emotionally available."

"I want you, and I'm here, right now." Slater threw up his hands. "I don't know what else to say."

"Are you going to … smoke me?"

"If that's what you want."

Pulling off his gauntlets, Andy got up and sat on the edge of the bed. "Get on … your knees."

Slater knelt in front of him and fished his cock out of his boxer shorts. He was already chubby. He took him into his mouth, and Andy quickly got hard. As Slater worked him, Andy cuffed him on the side of the head, a sharp blow with his fist. He ignored it, and Andy struck him again, a sharp knuckle to the temple.

Slater's instinct was to bite him, or slap his face, but he struggled to suppress his anger. No way was he going to give Andy the easy way out, physical pain to match the emotional pain he'd inflicted, an excuse to throw him out for good. He worked him harder, and soon Andy came, his whole body thrashing.

Once he'd caught his breath, Andy stretched out. "Get up here."

Climbing up beside him, Slater lay back as Andy worked to unbuckle his belt and pop his fly. He knew better than to try to help. Eventually Andy pulled his cock out, and stroked him with his iron grip. Andy mashed their mouths together, and Slater strained into him. He stuck his nose in Andy's hair, inhaling the heady scent of his sweat, and then climaxed.

He grabbed Andy's wrist to make him stop, but he didn't, not right away, inflicting as much discomfort as he could until Slater forcibly pulled his hand off.

"Fuck," Slater roared.

Andy rolled away from him. "You owe me three … hundred bucks. Leave it on my desk on … your way out."

Still panting, Slater eyed him sidelong, then sat up, and buttoned his fly, and buckled his belt. Peeling the bills from his wad of cash, he set them on his desk. Andy was facing away from him. Watching him for a moment, he wanted to say something. But there was nothing he could say.

Walking out, he felt a lump in his throat. How had his personal life gotten so goddamn complicated?

SIXTEEN

NOSING THE THUNDERBIRD INTO his garage, Slater climbed out and waited for the door to roll down. He didn't need to go upstairs, and instead walked to the armored cabinet next to the sink at the end of the garage bay. It looked like a basic office-supply sheet-metal box, but it was really a gun safe, designed to hide in plain view. He didn't have any firearms, but he kept his illicit tech in here, mostly the stuff he got from Svetlana.

He hauled out the heavy key binder, pages and pages of little pockets with standard hardware-store keys, along with Svetlana's lock reader to tell him which one to use. Loading both into a duffel bag, he heaved it into the trunk of the Thunderbird.

Back at the cabinet, he unplugged the frequency jammer from its charging cable and tucked it into his satchel. A plastic box about the size and weight of a brick, it wasn't nearly as heavy as the keys, but he'd have to take it inside with him. As long as it was switched on, it would jam any wireless cameras or security-system components, but it would also knock every nearby phone and laptop and tablet off Wi-Fi and the cell network, and people tended to freak out when that happened.

He needed another vehicle tracker, and took one from the cabinet, then locked it, and put his satchel and the tracker into the vehicle's trunk. Once he was behind the wheel, he hit the button to roll up the garage door. Chila's address was about twenty minutes' drive, the navigation app told him, mostly on the 60.

Once he was on surface streets in her neighborhood, he found himself driving up into the tonier part of Montebello. In the hills the lots were bigger—sprawling ranch houses with multiple-car garages instead of the more crowded bungalows with little driveways down below.

Chila's dark-green Camry was parked in front of the garage, he saw as he drove past. Farther up the block he turned around, then pulled to the curb a few houses up, facing Chila's place. He spent some time assessing the house. There were no cameras on the garage, and on the far side of the driveway a tall hedge obscured any view of the vehicle from that direction. The blinds were drawn in the windows that he could see from here. Someone might see him if they drove by, but it was a quiet street. It was safe enough to put a tracker on her car.

Reaching into the backseat, he took a pair of the black latex gloves from the box and wriggled his hands into them, then pulled his blue ball cap low over his brow. He climbed out and opened the trunk, and grabbed the tracker, then wiped it carefully on his shirt to remove any prints that might be on it.

Gently closing the trunk, he strode toward the place, looking at the house across the street that faced Chila's garage. There were no cameras in view there either, and it was set well back from the curb, too far for a wide-angle security camera to get any detail on him. There were so goddamn many cameras nowadays that it was almost impossible to go unseen. But the flip side of all that footage was that somebody still had to bother to go through it, and unless something unusual went down, that was unlikely to happen.

Looking over his shoulder, he saw that the street was empty. He stepped into Chila's driveway and squatted between the hedge and the rear tire of the Camry. Reaching up into the wheel well, he couldn't find a spot where it would adhere. Were these damn things made entirely of plastic? He could feel sweat trickling down his scalp. Shifting position, he reached higher up. Finally the magnets found some steel, and he felt the satisfying tug as they attached.

Slater rose and glanced around. Nobody was watching him. He strode to the sidewalk and back to his car. He got it started and got the air blowing, then tossed his cap in the backseat, and peeled off the gloves, and pulled out his phone. He needed to talk to that idiot in Venice today, the one who called himself Il Capitano.

When he plugged the address for Novo Paradigm into the navigation app, it told him it was over an hour's drive from here.

"Fuck," he roared. His head still hurt, and his muscles ached, the ill effects of the sauce dragging through the afternoon. An hour in heavy traffic was the last thing he needed. Cranking the air up high, he got on the 60. The traffic was maddeningly slow through downtown, like it always was, and the trendy Venice neighborhood was busier today, but he found a street space for the Thunderbird half a block from Novo Paradigm's office.

As he walked back toward it, he saw that the line for the limeade stand stretched onto the sidewalk and around the corner. The crowd was blocking Novo Paradigm's doorway, and Slater growled "Coming through" as he elbowed his way between them.

The door was unlocked, and he trotted up the stairs. No one was on the front desk.

"Hello?" he called.

Il Capitano stepped out of the hallway, his brow furrowed. Today he wore a mustard-yellow jacket over a red vest. It seemed like a lot of clothes for a hot summer day. But the air-conditioning was up high—he'd adjusted it to suit the look he was working.

His eyes flicked over him. "Mr. Ibáñez. Come on back."

"Violet doesn't work Sunday?"

"She's only here some days. We don't really

follow traditional business hours."

"Of course not," Slater said. "Things are done a little differently around here. Because you've created a new paradigm."

Il Capitano smiled. "Exactly."

He stifled a skeptical retort and followed him into the hallway. The back office was bigger, and had the same blue-and-white styling with some wood accents. It really was a pleasing color scheme, with just enough blond wood that it looked clean but didn't feel sterile. The designer had done a good job. There were more of the abstract paintings here, and they were real, not prints, he saw as they walked past them.

Stepping over to the windows, Slater looked out at the boulevard. It wasn't a great view, just the facades of the facing buildings, the tired postwar construction tarted up with paint and flashy signage. Lots of vehicles and pedestrians were plying the street below. This strip wasn't pretty. Il Capitano had to be here for the location.

"It's a shame what you people did to this neighborhood," Slater said, still gazing out the window.

"What are you talking about?"

"You killed it with money. You called it a cultural crucible, but anyone who's doing anything creative can't afford to live here, or rent studio space, or even eat lunch around here." Slater turned to Il Capitano, sitting at his desk now. "You've turned it into Beverly by the beach."

He folded his hands on his desk. "I suspect you don't actually know what's going on in Venice."

"You can just call me a peasant, if that's what you were thinking," Slater said.

"That's not what I was thinking."

"The same thing happened to the Arts District. The people who create art are long gone. I know some artists who rent space in Hyde Park these days. I probably shouldn't tell you that. You'll kill that neighborhood too."

Il Capitano frowned and waved to the chair in front of his desk. "Why don't you have a seat?"

Slater looked it over. "Is this by one of those designers that only design people like?"

"It's the Eames plywood chair."

"It looks a little delicate." He gingerly sat down. "And predictably uncomfortable too. I guess that's one way to discourage lingering."

"Beauty trumps utility, don't you think?"

Slater pointedly looked around the office. "I'm not sure that's the word I'd use. Overall your space is a little boring. It makes me sad."

His expression hardened. "At your end of the economy, that would make sense. You can't really know what you're looking at."

"My end of the economy." He scoffed. "What is it with you people? I drive west of the 405 and everyone assumes I'm the help." Slater cocked his head. "You know, you don't seem Jewish."

"Why would you think I'm Jewish?"

"You have a Jewish name."

"It's actually a biblical name," Il Capitano said. "My parents are evangelicals."

"I'm sure he was name-checked in your bible,

but Hezekiah was a king. A direct descendant of David and the sagacious Solomon." Slater raised his voice. "He was Jewish."

His brow furrowed. "I'm not arguing with you."

"Why do you call yourself Il Capitano? Why not just 'the captain'? Nothing about you is Hispanic either."

"It's actually Italian. From commedia dell'arte."

"Is that a cartoon? Or a 'graphic novel'?" Slater waggled his fingers to put the phrase in air quotes.

"It's thousand-year-old Italian cultural heritage. Short plays with Harlequin, and Pierrot, and Columbine. One of the characters is Il Capitano. I'm not surprised you've never heard of it."

"I don't watch cartoons."

"It's not a cartoon," he said sharply, and rolled his chair closer to the desk. "So what kind of insurance issue necessitates you coming in here, and insulting me, and taking up my time?"

"We'll get to that. First tell me what you do here. Your website made it sound like money laundering."

Il Capitano laughed, his voice deep, and sat back. "I know it must seem complicated. We leverage crypto instruments to facilitate entertainment industry activity around the world."

"You mean cryptocurrency. Is that the root of your business?"

"Among other assets, yes."

"What other assets?"

He gestured vaguely. "NFTs. Have you heard of those? They're mentioned in the mainstream media sometimes."

"And you buy and sell crypto for the entertainment business?" Slater said.

"We facilitate instant transactions unfettered by international borders."

"Again, that sounds like money laundering."

Il Capitano grinned. "I'm not doing anything wrong."

"Tell me about your relationship with Woody Newkirk."

He raised his eyebrows. "I'm a busy man, Mr. Ibáñez, and it's starting to feel like you're wasting my time. Unless you're going to explain what kind of insurance issue you're working on, I think we're finished."

"I think I've had enough of your condescending guff."

Slater stood up and walked around the desk. Alarm in his eyes, Il Capitano rolled backward in his chair. It was always the same thing with these birds. Angry and afraid at the same time. Leaning in, Slater slapped him, rapidly left and right, a powerful kovac.

The back of Il Capitano's chair slammed into a cabinet. "You fucking psycho. That's assault."

"You'll take it and you'll like it." Slater leaned in, and batted his hand away, and slapped him again.

"I'm calling the cops."

Slater stepped back and put his hands on his hips. "Do you have much experience in dealing with them? At my end of the economy, I know exactly how to talk to cops. I'll tell them you came at me first, and curiously, there are no cameras in here to dispute that." He gestured to the ceiling.

Glaring at him, his face red, Il Capitano was holding his cheek. "Asshole."

Slater leaned on the cabinet, looming over him. "What is it you people say? Move fast, break things? I will break your waspy little nose if you don't tell me about Woody Newkirk."

"He was a potential client," he said quickly. "He wanted to do events. We talked about me investing in them."

"What kind of events?"

"Concerts, parties, club nights. He found a venue willing to take payment in crypto, and I helped him figure that out."

"Did you invest with him?"

"We didn't get to that point. I actually saw him yesterday. I told him then that it wasn't going to work. It's not the right business for me. I need bigger margins."

"What about Greenleaf?"

"Is Greenleaf your insurance client?" Il Capitano said. "I know it's downtown. It's where Woody's performing, but it's not his event. Someone else is running club nights there. I don't know who. I'm not involved."

Slater believed him, he decided, and stood erect. This guy was no professional lowlife. The first hint of getting leaned on and he sang like a mockingbird.

Slater flashed his palms. "How difficult was that? All that tsuris."

"Maybe I will charge you with assault."

"You can try, but how much scrutiny of your business are you up for? I know a woman who works in the Department of Financial Regulation. She might be interested in looking over your books."

Slater could see doubt creeping into his eyes.

"Fuck you."

"No thanks," Slater said. "You're way too complicated, Il Capitano."

He strode toward the hallway, and down the stairs, and pushed his way through the string of idiots waiting to pay twelve bucks for a paper cup of sugar water. When he climbed into the Thunderbird, he got the air blowing, then checked on Chila's car. The tracker was online, showing a green circle around Chila's house and several of the neighboring ones. The accuracy was imprecise, but the implication was clear—the Camry was still at her place.

On the 10 headed east, Slater thought about Il Capitano. It was a useless lead. The guy didn't know much more about Woody than Slater already did. Maybe it was an insight that Woody wanted to promote his own events—the logical expansion of his business, from performing to promoting, and he didn't have enough capital of his own to make it happen.

He doubted Il Capitano was going to tattle on him, but it was still possible. White privilege made people act in irrational ways. Hopefully once he'd simmered down, and considered the full cost, he'd let it go.

Slater pushed it out of his mind and glanced at

the clock. He had time to hit Doris's yard. When he finally got through downtown, he exited the freeway into hilly Mount Washington and pulled into her driveway.

Doris's Buick was here, but her stupid boyfriend's stupid Boxster wasn't, thankfully. Albert. He scoffed at the thought of him. He wasn't afraid of that guy, but he was afraid of the repercussions when he eventually punched him in the face. He was such a dick-smack that it was all but inevitable.

As he climbed out, the heat struck him. It was past the hottest part of the day, but it was still sweltering and muggy. He walked to the side gate and into the backyard.

There was always something that needed doing here, and summer was the season of rapid growth. He had to triage. Assessing the ornamentals, and the fruit trees, and the rosebushes, he saw that the roses needed work the most urgently—he had to deal with the suckers.

Stepping into the little shed, he pulled on a pair of work gloves and grabbed a set of pruning shears and a claw hammer. He knelt at the base of a rosebush and yanked hard on the sucker, stripping it right off, and then pounded the newly stripped bark with the hammer, landing a dozen solid blows. As he started on the next one, Doris stepped outside. Slater sat back and called a greeting to her.

"What's with the hammer?" She put her hands on her hips. "Are you working out some aggression?"

"There are bud cells that will grow into more suckers. Smashing them will stop that. The bush can handle it. It'll be healthier without them."

"I know you know what you're doing," she said. "I adored Pike, by the way."

"He's back in Albuquerque."

"I'm just so happy you found someone to romance."

"I'm not sure where it's going," Slater said. "Although we did use the *l* word."

"How sweet." Doris laughed. "That seems like a fitting development in your narrative complex."

"It's hard to be objective about it," he said. "It feels like being hit by a cyclone. You know those mini whirlwinds you see out in the Mojave or in the Central Valley? *Bam*, I'm caught up in it, and twisted in every direction, and completely disoriented."

"At least there's movement. I was worried you were in a rut."

"You don't need to worry about stuff like that."

"I'm your mother. Worrying is a major part of the job." She gestured to the ornamentals. "Albert wondered about the mustard plants. When they flowered he thought they were weeds, but you've got them in neat rows. I said it had to be intentional."

Slater waggled the hammer. "If that man starts pulling out my plantings, I'll break his fingers."

"He didn't pull out anything," she said, and waved an arm. "Is mustard not a weed?"

"Planting it between the showier stuff attracts insects that eat the insects that eat the pretty things. The other alternative is spraying a bunch of pesticides. Why would I do that when nature already has a way to handle it?"

"There are a lot of insects," she said. "It always looks so lively over there."

"That's a sign that your yard is healthy," Slater said. "It's like with people. Diversity is a strength. They're not the kind of bugs that'll bother you."

"I'll let him know."

"Tell Albert to keep his grubby paws off the yard. He should stick to amputations and pushing opioids."

"That's not what he does. He's a knee surgeon."

"Have you seen him at work?" Slater demanded. "You don't actually know what he does."

She waved dismissively. "Have you had lunch? I'll make you a sandwich. I've got some of that fake turkey."

As she went inside, Slater dug out his phone and checked the tracking app. Chila was still home.

Once he'd pounded out all the suckers on the rosebushes, he went back to the shed and carried out a bag of horse manure. Kneeling beside the bed of artichokes, he massaged the redolent stuff into the soil, a handful at a time. Getting his hands into the earth always had a calming effect. It gave him something to think about besides Pike, and the feeling of his warm skin, and the way his pits smelled, and how he slept with his mouth half open.

Eventually he carried the manure back to the shed, and put the tools away, and slapped the dirt off his knees. Walking to the back door, he stepped into the house and washed up, then sat with Doris at the dining table to eat.

"So when are you seeing your man again?" she

said, gesturing with half a sandwich.

"He's coming out Wednesday."

"All that commuting is going to get expensive."

"It's so worth it. And don't ask me if I'm going to shack up with him. No way am I moving out there. I went for a weekend—he has a nice place, but it's not for me."

"Plus you just bought that house."

"I don't think I can be a desert rat," Slater said.

"I get it. You're an Angeleno."

After they'd eaten, Doris rose and cleared their plates. Slater checked his phone. Chila's car was finally moving.

He stood up. "I have to go."

"You should change your pants," Doris said.

"Do I smell?"

"Like a stable. Personally I don't mind, but if you've got meetings. That lovely shirt is thoroughly sweat-drenched too."

"I should have brought a change of clothes." He leaned in to kiss her. "Love you. Sorry about the horse manure."

"Like you said, it's totally worth it. I have the nicest yard in town."

As he climbed into the Thunderbird and got the air blowing, he couldn't really smell himself, but he'd been working with the fertilizer for a while. The linen shirt showed his sweat in dramatic dark damp spots, he saw, tilting the rearview down to look at it. He looked like hell. Cranking up the air, he backed into the street, then navigated to the 5 and headed to Montebello.

SEVENTEEN

NCE SLATER WAS ON Chila's street, he parked up the block from her house. There were no vehicles in the driveway. It was still risky—there might be cars in the garage and people inside. He didn't know if she had a family, but it was a reasonable assumption that a house that big would have more than one person living in it.

Checking his phone for the tracker on Chila's car again, he saw that it was in Commerce, at a big-box store. That was at least twenty minutes' drive from here. He pulled on a pair of the latex gloves, and the blue ball cap low over his brow, and climbed out. From the trunk he retrieved his satchel, and flipped it open to switch on the frequency jammer. It's blue LED was extremely bright, even in daylight, as a reminder not to forget it was illegally disrupting everyone's connectivity. Slinging the satchel onto his shoulder, he grabbed the lock reader. Its bulk was mostly the length of wire attached to the key-shaped probe, and he palmed it as he walked toward the house.

The front door looked disused. Like most people, Chila used the one closest to the driveway. It had a doorbell, and he pressed it, and heard the faint chime inside. Listening, there was no sound of movement within. Pounding on the door with the heel of his fist, he rang the bell again, and listened.

Pulling out his phone, he attached the lock-reading probe to it, and Svetlana's app popped up, presenting a black screen with the word "готов." Kneeling in front of the lock, he shifted his satchel onto his back and slid the probe in. The screen went red and displayed "ошибка." He didn't know what the word meant, but it wasn't working.

Slater pulled the probe out, and took a breath, wiping the sweat off his brow with the back of his hand. Sliding it in again, he adjusted the position, rotating it and sliding it out slightly. Sometimes it just took finesse. This time it worked, displaying a green screen with a lone number: 023.

He detached the cable from his phone and pocketed it, then walked back to his car and opened the trunk. Flipping through the binder of keys, 023 was near the front, and he slipped it out of its pouch.

When he got back to Chila's door, he rang the bell again, and listened, just in case, then tried the ghost key in the deadbolt. It twisted easily, and he felt the bolt retract. He pulled his cap low over his eyes, and opened the door, and stepped inside. This was the kitchen. There was no alarm tone, and no panel here. He strode into the foyer and the front door to check, but there was no alarm panel here either. If there were, he'd quickly have to abort. No cameras either, it seemed, at least not obvious ones.

"Gas company," he called out, walking back to the kitchen. "We're investigating a gas leak. You need to clear the building." He listened but there was no response.

Taking a deep breath, he slid the ghost key into his pocket, and shifted his cap higher on his head. There was no guarantee he wasn't being observed by a hidden camera, but it seemed less likely now, and he flipped open his satchel and switched off the frequency jammer. If he left it running any longer, the neighbors would start calling the fire department.

The place was tidy, he saw, sticking his head into the living room, and had decent furniture and new-ish appliances. The hallway had dark wood wainscotting. It was a nice place, and probably a stretch on an insurance clerk's salary, but maybe someone else in the family had money.

Opposite the living room was an office, with a big desk under the window. It was a beautiful antique, with carved ornaments at the corners, like the art deco pieces Etta had rented for their office. This one was larger and looked spendier. The desks in his office were what the clerical staff would have used back in the day, but this was a desk for a vice president.

A laptop sat folded closed on the blotter. It was unlikely he'd be able to get into that. He should have brought a keystroke logger. He had one that hid in a USB port and reported back to him remotely. Once Chila punched in her password, he could come back and access the computer at his leisure. Why hadn't he thought to bring it? Chila was unemployed, so her primary computer was going to be in her house, and this was likely it. He'd have to settle for a look at the paperwork instead.

Setting his satchel on the floor, he sat behind the desk and pulled open the drawers. One of them had vertical files, and he dug through them, his latex-clad fingers making it quick work. The folders were labeled: TAX FORMS, RECEIPTS, MORTGAGE. The one that made his pulse quicken was marked WOODROW HASSAN. He pulled it out and flipped it open.

The first sheet was a printout of a web page, with a banner at the top that read STATE CONTROLLER'S OFFICE, and under that UNCLAIMED PROPERTY. Scanning the other pages in the folder, he soon put together the story. A life insurance company from Iowa had been unable to locate a beneficiary: Woodrow Hassan. After a couple of months, the company turned over the policy payout funds to the California state controller, as Cali was where the policy had been set up. The dough had been sitting there unclaimed for several years. Slater flipped to the next sheet. This was a record of the funds from the state controller's website. He had to look closer, to make sure he was understanding it correctly. It said the policy had paid out over three million bucks.

Slater stared at the page. This was it—this is what Chila was after, why she wanted to find Woody. Pulling out his phone, he photographed all the pages, from the first sheet, one by one, and tucked them back into the folder.

As he was about to put the folder back in the drawer, he heard the kitchen door rattle open, and voices in conversation, a man and a woman. He froze. One of them was Chila's voice. How had she gotten here so quickly?

Slater rose and stepped quietly over to the room's open door, and flattened himself against the wall in the shadows behind it. No way was he going to let himself get caught. Maybe no one would come in here. He took deep deliberate breaths, working to slow his breathing, his mind racing to formulate an escape plan. If they went upstairs, he reasoned, he could slip out the kitchen door. He could feel the sweat on the back of his neck.

His satchel, he remembered. No matter what, he couldn't leave that here. He stepped lightly across the room to the desk, where he'd left it, and gingerly lifted the strap around his neck, sliding the bag onto his back.

He was halfway to the door when a guy with dark hair walked into the room, and flipped on the lights, and turned toward the desk. Slater froze, and their eyes met.

"Intruder," the guy shouted, and lunged at him, and snapped a hand into his face, striking Slater's nose.

Slater's ball cap flew off, and he shoved the

guy away. He was wiry, and moving fast, but Slater managed to punch his chin, fast and light, just hard enough to get some movement. As he involuntarily twisted away, Slater grabbed his wrist, and shoved his arm up his back, and the guy yelped in pain. Slater put his other hand around his throat and pulled him close. He clawed at Slater's forearm with his free hand but couldn't budge it.

"Stop moving or I'll dislocate your arm," Slater growled in his ear.

He went slack, and Slater held firm. His nose throbbed, and he could feel blood on his upper lip now, leaking out of his nostril. The guy had landed a solid blow.

Chila stepped into the room, her eyes wide. "What the fuck are you doing here?"

He glared at her over the guy's shoulder. "You lied to me, Chila."

"You know this *pendejo*?" he said.

Slater pushed his arm higher, and he yelped again. He could smell his sweat, and feel the pulse in his neck, and the firmness of his butt pressed against his thigh. The guy was a little lean but totally fuckable.

"You're bleeding," Chila said.

"Thanks to this hooligan."

"I'm calling the cops."

"Be my guest," Slater said, "but I'll tell them you invited me here. I have evidence of our fiduciary relationship, remember? When you paid me through the bank. Can you see now why cash is always the better option? You left a trail."

"How do you know him?" the guy shouted.

"We work together," Chila said, and louder, "you broke into my house."

"I didn't break anything. The door was unlocked."

"Bullshit," the guy said. "You're wearing gloves."

"That's for a skin condition. More important right now is what's in that file behind me on the desk."

"Let him go," Chila said.

"Only if he's not going to start a brawl."

"*Mijo*, go upstairs."

"We need to call the cops."

"No cops," she snapped. "You do as I say."

Slater spoke into his ear. "If you come at me again, brother, I will break your arm."

As he released his grip, Slater shoved him away. The guy took a step, then shot him a burning look, his lip curled in a sneer as he rotated his arm and massaged his shoulder.

"Christ, how old are you?" Slater demanded. He hadn't gotten a good look at him when the guy attacked him.

"Nineteen." He frowned. "Asshole."

At least he hadn't been brawling with a minor. Slater wiped at the blood on his lip, then peeled off the latex gloves.

"Get out," Chila said, waving at the guy.

As he walked past her, she smacked him on the back of the head. He flinched but didn't protest. Chila moved to close the door after him.

"I see you like them green," Slater said. "Personally I wouldn't go quite that young, but hey, smoke 'em if you've got 'em."

"Eddy is my son, you dipshit." Stepping over to him, she punched him on the shoulder.

"Knock it off with the static." Slater took a step back and rubbed his arm.

"Goddamn *pocho*, breaking into my house," Chila said, scowling at him. "Do you have any idea what a violation that is?"

"Aren't *pochos* Mexicans? I'm not Mexican. None of my people are Mexican. My father was from Central America."

"You know I could call the cops. We caught you dead to rights. Eddy will back me up."

"I'd rather focus on Woodrow Hassan's three million dollars. From what I just read, it's not actually yours to give away. That right belongs to the Honorable Lindsay Nguyen, state controller." Slater gestured to the desk. "I think I might have voted for that sap. I wonder if your friends in blue would be interested to hear about that? I mean the fraud you're plotting, not who I voted for."

Chila shifted uncomfortably on her feet, and furrowed her brow. He could see the wheels turning.

"Does Montebello have its own cops," Slater said, raising his eyebrows, "or is it sheriff's department?"

"I wish you'd wipe the blood off your face." She stepped over to the credenza, and yanked a tissue out of the box, and handed it to him.

Slater wiped off his upper lip and blew his nose.

"I admit that I should have told you the whole story," Chila said, and folded her arms.

"You didn't tell me any of it," Slater said, raising his voice. "You lied to my face. What was your plan for Woodrow Hassan?"

"He doesn't know about that money, Slater. That's why it's unclaimed. I really do want to help him get his hands on it."

"What's in it for you?"

"I thought he might be grateful for the information, and pay me a small finder's fee."

"The penny-ante stuff doesn't wash, sister. You dropped a grand on me without even blinking. That tells me there's a lot more in it for you. You thought you could con him into signing it over somehow. He'd give you power of attorney, or you'd impersonate him. Your plan was to get most or all of the dough for yourself."

"It's not that far out, is it?" Chila said. "I'll cut you in. Ten percent if you can find Woodrow. That's three hundred grand in your pocket. You could buy yourself all the crystal meth in WeHo."

"That's an interesting starting point. How were you planning to con him?"

She frowned. "It's not a con. I was going to explain that I was in the insurance field, which is true, and that I could get him some money if he signed some forms."

"So you'd give him ten percent and keep the rest."

"I was thinking he'd probably be thrilled to get a hundred grand, but I'm not greedy."

Slater waved at the room. "Are you still paying the mortgage on this place?"

"What's that got to do with anything?"

"Why do you need so much dough? It's obviously not for upkeep. Your things are a little …" He paused for effect, and looked around the room. "Cheap."

Anger flashed in her eyes, and she stepped toward him, and slapped him hard. Slater shoved her away.

"Show some restraint, woman."

Chila adjusted her jacket. "Fuck you."

"No thanks," Slater said. "And you're getting ahead of yourself. You need me to find the guy, and that's worth a lot more than ten percent."

Her eyebrows shot up. "Twenty, but that's my limit."

"Now that I know about the situation, why wouldn't I just take all the gravy for myself and cut you out completely?"

"It was my idea," she said, raising her voice. "I'm the one with the plan. You need me to work the guy."

"Are you sure about that?"

She gestured wildly. "You're a field monkey. You don't know about insurance and all the forms and how to set up the paperwork."

"Nobody's going to get anything if I can't find him."

"So find him. Nothing's changed."

"Except that I get half of whatever you take."

Chila glared at him. She knew she had no other choice.

"Fine," she said flatly.

"And if you try to cut me out," Slater said, "I will burn you to the ground."

"I said fine." She threw up her hands. "Let's get to work."

As she opened the office door, Slater snatched his ball cap off the floor and followed her out. Eddy was standing in the kitchen, his feet apart, brow furrowed, murder in his eyes. Slater could see his pecs through his shirt, and the musculature of his legs in his pants.

Slater jutted his chin. "Spread out."

"You're a damn bully," Eddy said.

"You came at me, and bloodied my nose, remember?"

"I got one punch in, then you got hold of my arm. It happened fast. I can't quite figure out how you did that."

"Come outside. I'll show you. It's not that difficult."

"You don't need to be teaching him that," Chila said.

Eddy scowled at her. "Why not? I should be able to defend myself."

"You've got the basics," Slater said. "You just need a little guidance."

Chila waved an arm. "What is it with men and violence?"

"You just hit me, twice," Slater said, "and I saw you smack Eddy upside the head. You of all people can't claim fisticuffs are gender-specific."

Pulling his cap on, he walked out the kitchen door. Outside the long shadows of the end of the day stretched across the neighborhood, the last golden light blazing on the houses higher up the hill. It was finally getting a little cooler. There was a black pickup parked at the curb in front of the yard, but no sign of the Camry.

Standing in the driveway, Slater set his satchel on the concrete as Eddy stepped out.

"Were you riding today?" Eddy said.

"You mean horses? Why would you say that?"

"When you were manhandling me, you smelled like a horse."

"I wasn't manhandling you. It was self-defense." He shifted his cap back on his head. "That punch of yours succeeded mostly because you're fast. You need more than speed."

"Like more muscle. Nature hasn't really given me that option."

"It's not about bulk. It's about what you do with it. Those musclebound types aren't really dangerous, right, because their bulk makes them slow. Martial arts masters don't have the bulging muscles but they can croak you with one punch."

"So if I don't need bulk," Eddy said, "what do I need?"

"Agility, and power. For power you have to channel the force. From your waist, into your shoulder, and then into your fist. In a line." Slater demonstrated by punching the air, first at normal speed and then in slow motion. "Can you see the flow? Pelvis to shoulder to fist."

Eddy tried it, and Slater stepped closer, and made an adjustment to his elbow.

"You lose power with the lateral movement. Remember the flow. Keep it in a direct line."

He practiced a few times, first slowly, then at full speed.

"I can feel it," he said. "It definitely intensifies the force."

"Now hit my shoulder," Slater said.

Eddy did, slowly at first, then at full speed, but only tapped his arm.

"You have good form, and we know you've got speed," Slater said. "Try again, and don't hold back."

This time Eddy's blow spun him sideways. Slater laughed and rubbed his arm. Chila was watching them, standing in front of the kitchen door, her arms folded.

"You've got it."

"How did you get hold of my arm?" Eddy said.

"That's about agility. I knew where your wrist was going to be because I rabbit-punched you. I knew you'd turn away. A lot of it is just knowing what your opponent's next move will be, then reacting appropriately. In this case it was about moving to intercept your wrist."

"I couldn't pull out of it."

"It's an unnatural position," Slater said. "It doesn't matter how strong your arms are, you won't be able to break free."

"Show me how you did that."

"Punch my jaw with a right hook." Slater narrowed his eyes. "Not for real."

Eddy delivered a slow right hook, and Slater rotated his head.

"See where my left arm goes as my head turns?" he said. "I'm not thinking about my arm, but you can. Just reach across with your left and grab my wrist while I'm not focused. Try it again."

As Eddy mimed a right hook, Slater rotated away, and Eddy grabbed his left wrist.

"Now twist it up my back and pull me close," Slater said. "Your other arm goes around my collar."

Eddy shoved his arm hard, and flattened his palm on Slater's clavicle.

"You get it," Slater said. "That's what I did. No need to hurt me."

"You know I really want to, though," Eddy said, his breath hot on Slater's neck. He squeezed his torso with his arm, holding him firm a moment longer, then let go.

Before he turned around, Slater rotated his shoulder and swung his arm, as if Eddy really had hurt him, and with his other hand adjusted his crotch, glad that he was facing the end of the driveway so neither Chila nor Eddy could see what was going on. Getting manhandled by this guy was putting lead in the pencil.

"I work in a restaurant," Eddy said. "The people who need punching are the angry drunks who pick fights."

"Drunks are easy."

"They're usually a little slow, but not always."

"You've already got the speed advantage," Slater said, "but drunks are also top-heavy. Let me show you. Pretend to be a drunk taking a swing at me."

Eddy threw a slow punch, and Slater crouched,

and lunged at him, wrapping his arms around his thighs. He pulled back and stood erect.

"If I kept going, I'd easily toss you on your ass. It's hard to do to someone who's sober and has good balance, but that move will always take down a drunk. They don't get up very quickly either."

"How did you learn all this?" Eddy said.

"Mostly life experience. You could take a self-defense class. Did you ever do martial arts?"

Eddy shook his head.

"When you came at me it felt like you knew some of that stuff," Slater said. "You should look into it. Karate, maybe. It's straightforward. Go for one without any props or weapons. Those blade ones are just impractical."

"I get it. You can't really walk around with a sword."

Slater looked toward the house and saw that Chila was gone. He picked up his satchel. "I have to go."

"What were you talking about with my mother? Are you in some kind of business together?"

"You'll have to take that up with her."

Eddy raised his eyebrows. "You did break into our house."

"Or did she give me the key and tell me to wait for her inside? Nothing's broken."

"She was surprised to see you."

"Maybe she forgot she'd done that." Slater shrugged. "Later, tough guy."

He walked out to the street, and down the block, and climbed into the Thunderbird. On his phone the tracking app showed that Chila's car was still in Commerce at the big-box store. Maybe she'd left it there for repairs, or new tires, and Eddy had brought her home. That was likely his pickup out front.

When he got back to his house, he climbed the stairs to the kitchen and poured his ration into a tumbler. It was a little early, but the sun was long gone, and he was in for the night. Maybe it would finally take the edge off his hangover. Flicking the room lights off, he propped open the French doors and then stretched out on the sofa. That first satisfying sip made him cough a little from the heady fumes, and he set the tumbler on the carpet, gazing out at the glittering towers of the Financial District in the distance.

He'd made a stupid assumption about Chila's whereabouts. It had been doubly stupid to let himself get caught. It could have gone much worse—at least he had a version of her story now that mostly rang true. Things were definitely coming together.

Slater took another sip and smiled to himself. Sometimes cons made the biggest chumps. What a sucker Chila was to think he was going to collaborate with her to swipe that insurance payout. He was going to make sure she never saw a dime of Woody's money.

EIGHTEEN

S LATER WOKE IN HIS bed, wincing at the bright daylight streaming in the sheers. Grabbing his phone, he pulled on a pair of boxers and went up to the kitchen. His head didn't hurt, he realized. That was always a good sign.

After he'd had some coffee, and ate a couple of handfuls of the dry cereal Rosa had bought, he went back down to get dressed. A dark shirt, he decided. Yesterday's jeans had a distinct whiff of the stable, so he dumped them in the bottom of the closet and pulled on a clean pair. Hustling down to his garage, he drove downtown and parked in the surface lot behind Andy's building.

When he knocked on his door, Andy pulled it open and gave him a pointed once-over, then turned to walk inside.

"Is your dick itchy?" Andy said.

"What?"

"Is that why you come … around here? To scratch it? Because your true love is … out of town?" He sat in his desk chair and swiveled to face Slater.

Breathing hard, Slater put his hands on his hips. "You don't have to tell me I'm trash. I know that already. I come here because you're my friend, and you're hot. I like looking at you, and I like talking to you, even when you're upset with me."

"How hot am I, exactly?"

"Totally freaking hot. Level ten. People get in fender-benders when you roll down the street because they can't take their eyes off you." He gestured impatiently. "You know this. Sometimes I just think about you and I get chubby."

Andy nodded, and cracked a smile. It was the first time Slater had seen that in a long time.

"Good answer. So what … do you need?"

"I have tech industry questions." Slater pulled a chair out from the little table under the windows, and twisted it around, and sat on it backward, facing Andy. "A guy says he's facilitating entertainment industry transactions using cryptocurrency and NFTs. Does that sound like money laundering?"

"Not necessarily," Andy said. "What kind of transactions?"

"It's on his website. You can read about it."

He recited the company name, and Andy swiveled to his computer, and pulled on his gauntlets, and studied the screen. Eventually he spoke.

"It sounds like they're trying to … displace banks and credit companies." Andy turned to him. "Banks are notoriously slow at … moving money around. Crypto transactions are much faster."

"Is that why a company would sign up to use his service?"

"That seems likely. For this Novo Paradigm, I'm sure the … goal is percentages."

"The company is one guy," Slater said. "He calls himself Il Capitano."

"From commedia dell'arte?"

"That's what he said."

"Funny. The Il Capitano character is … kind of a stuffed shirt."

"I've only seen it a few times," Slater said. "They used to perform it in the park behind LACMA in the summer. Doris would drag me over there so she could mack on highbrow guys."

"Aw. Sweet Doris."

"This guy is kind of nebbishy. More like the sneaky character with the checkered outfit."

"Harlequin," Andy said.

"Right. Which one was the liar?"

"Brighella."

"Also an appropriate model for this loser."

"Any financial services business gets a cut of the … transactions they handle. They charge a percentage on … everything. Crypto transactions don't actually cost … anything, so it's all gravy."

"So crypto is just a new way to do regular business?"

"Big picture," Andy said, "crypto is a grift, and NFTs … are a grift."

"In this situation, is Il Capitano the grifter or the mark?"

"If he's moving crypto around, his grift … is more likely about those percentages. Him getting his cut. It's … actually a clever way to make money on a wildly unstable asset. You don't … have to buy a bunch of it yourself. Even if it loses … half its value, you still get your slice."

Slater nodded. "Interesting."

"Or Il Capitano might actually … believe it's the way of the future, and that he's helping create a new paradigm."

"Which makes him the mark."

"It's hard to say. The richest people in the world … are the ones taking a cut of financial trans-actions. That's really what … banking is all about, and the credit card business."

"Different topic," Slater said. "What do you know about unclaimed property, and the state controller?"

Andy pulled off his gauntlets. "Well, it's cov-ered in state law. If a bank or … insurance company can't find an account owner or a policy beneficiary, they … turn it over to the state. In the old days the companies would just … keep it. The unclaimed property law was written to address that. But it's like an … arms race. The banks countered with new … terms about fees. Nowadays when you sign up for an account they … make you agree to inactive account fees. In effect they can still … seize aban-doned accounts by charging fees until it's empty. But some stuff still gets turned … over to the state. The state controller has a list of … unclaimed assets. I know it's online."

"Lindsay Nguyen."

"I thought she was the mayor of Garden Grove or … Westminster or someplace down there."

"It's because of term limits," Slater said. "Politicians have to jump around like musical chairs."

"There are companies that specialize … in tracking down people who don't know they're owed. They ask for … ten percent, but of course they're not legally entitled to anything."

Slater stood up. "Do I need to pay you for the consult?"

"I'll roll it into the next job."

"Can I kiss you, or are you too pissed at me?"

Andy chuckled. "Bring it in, cowboy."

Leaning in, Slater put a hand on his shoulder, and met his mouth, savoring the warm intensity. When he pulled back, he held Andy's gaze for a moment. "Bye, beautiful."

———•———

As Slater climbed into the Thunderbird, his phone buzzed in his pants. He dug it out to check—Woody.

"How did it go with the twink?" Slater said, and started the engine to get the air blowing.

"We set up a date for next week."

"Right on." Slater set the phone in its dash mount. "Was it all about twelve-step, or all about mayonnaise?"

"A little of both," Woody said. "We talked about other things."

"Artémise?"

"You were right—she's embroiled in quite the scandal. People are furious. It's a whole thing."

"That's basically her job description," Slater said, pulling into the street. "To generate gossip. Her music is secondary."

"We also talked about reality TV. He's really into that one where they give women surgery and a makeover, and at the end they all look like the same person."

"That sounds like a barn-burner. I take it Lars is a renaissance man."

"I wonder if I might be tired of him already."

"The dick wants what the dick wants," Slater said. "At least you'll get to tap that pasty little butt."

"It's odd, don't you think? Who you're attracted to and who you're compatible with don't always overlap."

"I hear you, brother."

"Are you around today? I thought we might do a nooner."

"You need some distraction until Lars is available?"

"I kind of liked your energy," Woody said. "It was pretty great sex. I like your body, even though you're not a gymbot."

"Are you sure you can deal with me? You were pissed about the way I handled that drunk."

"Paradoxically that actually added to your hotness."

"I'm on my way to my place now," Slater said.

"I have to go talk to Les at Greenleaf for a minute. I'll be there after that."

When he got to his house, upstairs in his bedroom, Slater changed into a white T-shirt. Guys liked that look, like a blank canvas that they could project their own stuff onto. A while later the doorbell rang, and he hustled downstairs, and pulled it open for Woody.

"I love that shirt," Woody said, and grinned. "It flatters your chest."

Slater led the way up to the bedroom, and turned to face him. Woody felt his pecs, then put his hands on his neck, and pulled him into a kiss. Slater mouthed his neck as he unbuttoned Woody's shirt, then slipped it off.

"Can I do you this time?" Woody said, his tone soft.

"I don't know, crooner. Can you?"

He chuckled. "Oh, yeah."

Woody unbuckled Slater's belt, and soon they were both naked. Woody straddled him on the bed, squeezing their cocks together. Slater quickly got hard. Reaching for the bedside table, Woody grabbed a condom, and rolled it on, then shifted closer, and pushed Slater's knees up. Breathing hard, he pressed his way into him. Slater winced with the intensity of it, and leaned into him, grasping the back of Woody's neck.

Starting slowly, Woody built up speed until he was pounding him, looming over him, and then came with a groan. He collapsed onto Slater, his skin warm and sweaty. Slater ran a hand over his back.

Eventually Woody pulled up, and shifted on his

side, and stroked Slater's cock.

"What do you want me to do?" he said.

"Exactly what you're doing." Slater put a hand on his shoulder, and pulled him close, exploring his mouth and then pressing his nose into his hair, inhaling his heady scent. Straining into Woody's fist, Slater came, then grabbed his arm to make him stop.

Woody lay back, and Slater dozed for a while, until his voice pulled him back to consciousness.

"Do you have anything to eat?"

"I can order takeout," Slater said. "How's Thai?"

Once he'd ordered, he set his phone aside and folded his arm over his eyes, dozing until the doorbell rang.

Jumping up, Slater pulled on his boxers, and grabbed his cash out of his jeans to tip the driver, and hustled down to the door.

"Soup's on," he called as he passed the bedroom, and carried the bag up to the kitchen.

Once he'd grabbed forks, he carried everything outside, wincing at the bright midday sun. When Woody came out, he was wearing only his underpants.

"What's with all the flowers?" Woody said. "Did you have a wedding up here?"

"They were for Reddy Kilowatt."

Woody nodded, pulling the lid off a takeout container. "That's a sweet gesture."

After they'd eaten, he pushed his plate away and sat back.

"I was thinking about that drunk who was

selling wolf tickets," Woody said. "How you went after him."

Slater stifled a sigh. This was what happened after the good part, after the sex and the food—the yapping, the complaining, the airing of grievances.

"I didn't go after anybody," he said. "I stopped an aggressive drunk idiot from attacking your bandmate. Sally. She acted like I was the problem. She's a damn ingrate."

"I should be used to the rough stuff, I suppose," Woody said, "working in bars and nightclubs. But it was a little shocking."

"On the phone today you implied that it turned you on."

"That's the difficult part. I feel like I should be repulsed by violence, end of story."

A bit of breeze had come up, and Slater set his plate on top of the bag the food had come in so that it wouldn't blow away.

"Did you take any history classes at college?"

Woody frowned. "How do you know I went to college?"

"Didn't you?"

"I did, but I didn't do social sciences."

"In all of human history," Slater said, "when someone wants to mess you up, or kidnap you, or croak you, the only way to stop it is to overpower the attacker with greater force. A sunny attitude and seeking middle ground never stopped a fist-fight, or a murder, or a war."

"That's a dark outlook."

"Reality is kind of dark." Slater watched him

for a moment. "It's not just about fistfights. Power can be brains, or the power of the state in the badge, or even the power of persuasion, like MLK had. Accomplishing anything worthwhile takes one of those. Brawn or brainpower."

"You're basically saying that you and MLK have the same role in the world."

"I know he had a better vocabulary than me," Slater said, "but I bet I've got a better left hook." He balled his fists and mimed a punch.

"There's something else, Slater." Woody shifted in his chair. "It's been bugging me. I want a straight answer."

Slater gestured impatiently.

"I talked to Les today. She said you came to Greenleaf the day before the opening. That's before I even met you. She remembered telling you about the hidden neon sign."

"So what?"

"So what the hell?" He leaned on the table. "Is it just a coincidence? I've been thinking about it. I'd say it's pretty damn unusual to pick up a guy in a thrift store. Were you stalking me?"

"If I explain it to you," Slater said, "you can't get pissed at me."

His brow furrowed. "Start talking."

"Full disclosure: I knew who you were when I saw you at the thrift store."

"You followed me there?" he demanded. "Why?"

"See, you're already upset. What happened to don't get pissed at me?"

Woody shook his head and sat back. "I don't

believe this. You're out of your damn mind."

"I hear that a lot."

"And violent, roughing up that drunk. Sally was right. What you're doing is crazy." Woody jabbed a finger at him. "Leave me out of it. I can't believe I hooked up with a fucking crazy person."

Woody got up and strode inside. After he'd waited long enough for him to get to the bedroom and start to get dressed, Slater picked up the cutlery and takeout containers and stepped in, carrying it all over to the kitchen. A minute later came the sound of footfalls descending from the bedroom, and then the front door slammed. He stood listening to the empty house. Why did people have to be so damn high-strung?

Once he'd put the leftovers in the Frigidaire, he threw out the empty containers and washed his hands. On the counter his phone buzzed, and he picked it up to check. The caller ID said "DOI." He knew who that was—the state agency that regulated his entire industry.

"Ibáñez," he said as he picked up.

"My name is Norris," a woman's voice said. "I'm with the Department of Insurance. We need to meet."

"Why's that?"

"We need to debrief you."

"What case is this about?" Slater said. "I work on a lot of different stuff."

"We can talk about that in detail face to face."

He scoffed. Such a bureaucrat. "OK. When do you want to see me?"

"As soon as possible," Norris said. "Can you come by our office?"

"You people are in Fort Ronnie? I guess I can come over there now."

NINETEEN

N HIS BEDROOM SLATER pulled on his jeans and a clean shirt, then went down to the garage, and drove to the Civic Center, parking the Thunderbird in a structure on Third.

Fort Ronnie was a massive pink monolith of an office building, put up in the darkest part of the 1980s. It had an official name as the city's primary state office building, but it looked like a fortress, and the people who had to work in it had given it that nickname.

When Slater walked in the main entrance, the bored-looking security guard staffing the metal detector heaved himself out of his chair and languorously waved him through. Nobody else was around so late in the day. Slater pulled out his keys and his phone and put them into a little tray, then stepped through the narrow frame of the detector. It started beeping at high volume.

"Slow down, son." The guard shuffled over to him and grabbed the hand wand.

Slater knew the drill, and turned to face him, spreading his feet apart and extending his arms. The guard waved the wand down his back, and along his arms, then over his chest. When it got to his crotch, it shrieked with a wild electronic squeal.

"And there it is," the guard said. "It's usually the belt buckle."

"Do you need me to take it off?"

"You're all good. On your merry way."

Slater scooped up his phone and his keys, and stuffed them back in his jeans as he walked toward the elevators. When he stepped off on the floor Norris had told him to come to, he found a counter with a woman in a gray jacket sitting behind it. She looked up expectantly as he approached.

"I have a meeting with Norris," Slater said.

"Follow me," she said, and rose.

She led him down a hallway and into a small room with three wooden chairs flanking a bare table.

"Have a seat," she said, and closed the door behind her.

Slater looked around the windowless space. There was one of these in every police station—an interrogation room. The only things missing were two-way glass and video cameras. Later he'd remember that this should have been his first clue that something was amiss.

Dropping into one of the chairs, he idly wondered if the door was locked from the outside. He was about to get up to try it when it flew open and a woman stepped in. Curvy, she wore a dark-blue suit and had myriad little dreads tied at the side of her head. Once she'd closed the door, she slapped a thin manila file folder on the table.

Slater folded his arms. "You must be Norris."

"Oh, don't get up," she said, and waved a hand as she sat across from him.

"Why would I get up? Are you a duchess or something? You should check your history book. This country stopped paying attention to the nobility after the revolution."

She was ignoring him, studying her phone screen.

"So what's this about?" Slater said.

"Hold on a minute." She held up a finger, not looking at him.

He could feel his heart pounding. The disrespect was intentional, he knew—a tactic intended to unnerve him and gain the upper hand. He could walk out right now. He wasn't being detained. No way did she have that power. But knowing that she was running a mind game on him made it easier not to react, and he was curious about this.

The door opened again, and a schlubby guy with a pencil mustache stepped in and closed it. Wearing an avocado-green suit, his hair was thinning, even though he was young for that, still in his twenties. He sat next to Norris, and set a little black device on the table, then pressed a button on it.

"I'll be recording this conversation," he said.

"The fuck are you?" Slater demanded.

The guy frowned. "The name is Titov. I'm also an investigator."

"I guess I'll be recording this conversation too," Slater said, and pulled out his phone, and started the audio recorder, and set it on the table in front of him.

"Is that really necessary?" Titov said.

"I'll holster mine if you holster yours, toots."

Norris finally tucked her phone into her jacket and met his gaze. "What do you know about unclaimed property?"

"Did you leave your tampons on the metro?" Slater said. "They're probably sitting in a box in an office somewhere. You should check the website."

Her expression didn't change. "Unclaimed property that's surrendered to the state. Bank accounts, retirement accounts, insurance payouts."

"My understanding is that it's the purview of the honorable Lindsay Nguyen. Not you saps."

"What's your involvement with unclaimed property cases?"

Slater chuckled and sat up. They couldn't have uncovered Chila's scheme. Not yet. She hadn't even made her first move.

"I have no involvement with anything like that," he said, and spread his palms. "Why do you ask?"

Her brow furrowed slightly as she studied him. Hopefully she was figuring out that he wasn't going to volunteer anything. Finally she spoke.

"An accusation has been made that you were angling to obtain someone else's unclaimed property."

"I'd call that a spurious accusation," Slater said. It had to be from Chila—nobody else knew anything about it. "What evidence do you have of any wrongdoing on my part? Besides inuendo, I mean."

Norris flipped open the file folder, and took out a sheet, and slid it over to him. A printout from a bank, Slater saw, dated last week. It detailed what Chila had paid him.

"For the recording," Norris said, "I'm handing Mr. Ibáñez a banking transaction record. It shows Mr. Ibáñez in receipt of one thousand dollars."

"You should also tell the recording who sent it," Slater said. "Isidra Suárez, currently unemployed and receiving benefits from the good people of California, formerly a clerk at Westside Title Guarantee. Also for the recording, I don't see anything on this page that says anything about unclaimed property." He slid the sheet back across to her.

Norris pulled her phone out of her jacket, and tapped at it, and set it on the table.

"This is a message you left for Ms. Suárez."

A tinny rendition of his own voice came through the phone's little speaker: *You'd better be dead, because if you just stood me up, I'll make you wish you were.*

"I would characterize that as a threat," Norris said, her gaze level.

"To me that doesn't seem threatening at all. It's just an expression of frustration at being disrespected." Slater frowned. "Actually I don't even think that's my voice. The message might have come from my number, but I loan my phone to various business associates on a regular basis, and also to a homeless individual who hangs out in the parking lot by my office. He likes to keep in touch with his mother, as much as he can in his addled condition, and I'm a generous person."

"This doesn't have to be adversarial, Mr. Ibáñez."

"So now you're the good cop?" Slater demanded. "You hauled me into a windowless room and started recording me. You're the one who brought the adversarial, sister."

Titov scowled. "Show some decorum."

Slater raised his eyebrows. "The stoic speaks." He gestured to him, then to her. "I like what you two got going. Black and white, female and male, good cop bad cop, ugly and uglier. It really gives me faith in the competency of our civil service."

"Why did Isidra Suárez send you a thousand dollars?" Norris said.

"She hired me to find someone. That was payment for my work."

"Who did she want you to find?" Titov said.

"Ask her. If you want me to get into the details of a confidential business arrangement, you can subpoena me and depose me under oath."

"Suárez says you blackmailed her because she gave you details about an unclaimed life insurance case," Norris said.

Slater had to laugh. "That makes no freaking sense. One, Lindsay Nguyen is pretty tits-out about unclaimed property. Anyone on the planet can see the full list on the controller's website. It's not Chila's proprietary information. And two,

Chila worked, past tense, in title insurance. That has nothing to do with life insurance." He sat back. "You need to ask yourselves, why was this wild aspersion made? Who's running the con? Who's actually being manipulated here?"

Folding her arms, Norris watched him, and pursed her lips.

"I know you birds can't actually charge me with anything," Slater said. "You're just fishing. E for effort, though."

"If you're not going to be forthcoming with us," Titov said, "we can make your life difficult at Cudahy Mutual. You probably work with Mark, or Della, is that right? I know them both. I can tell them you've been accused of blackmailing this woman."

"I'm amazed that you would utter that kind of threat on tape. You sound like a damn syndicate boss. It might not survive on your version of the recording, but it's on mine too." Slater tapped his phone. "Did that slip your mind?"

"It wasn't a threat," Titov said sharply.

"What evidence do you have besides what Chila told you? And why would you believe her?" He eyed Titov and frowned. "Unless you're sleeping with her. I mean, rock on if you're into older women, but she's got a son your age, in case you didn't know."

"I'm not sleeping with her," he said, raising his voice. "That would be totally inappropriate."

"Inappropriate like hauling me in here based on water-cooler gossip. You seem a little tightly wound, Titov. You should climb up on this pony." He pointed to his lap with both hands. "For the recording let it be known that I'm pointing at my crotch. I could bring some tranquility to your world."

"I'm married, you sleazeball."

"That doesn't bother me. I wouldn't mind if your wife watched us while I made a real man out of you."

"You're a fucking psycho," he said, his face reddening. "Chila was right about that."

Norris put her fist over her mouth, as if she were about to cough. She was trying not to laugh, he realized.

"You need to control your henchman's outbursts," Slater said to her. "I wish you people would show some decorum." He waved a hand. "Listen—to me it sounds like a he-said she-said type situation, and I call bullshit. You can either get someone to charge me with something, or you can go fuck yourselves." He leaned toward Titov and pointed a finger. "And if you interfere in any way with my income from Cudahy Mutual, I'll come after you for professional misconduct and defamation."

Rising, Slater scooped up his phone, and walked out, and headed to the elevators. His heart was still pounding when he climbed into his car. Had that really just happened? His office was just a few blocks away. Maybe Max was around. Even though he regularly wanted to punch the guy in the face, Max was level-headed, and a reasonable sounding board.

The lobby of their building was abandoned for the day, and when he got upstairs, as luck would have it, the lights were on, and Max was at his desk. Slater stuck his head into his office.

"You look a little frazzled," Max said, sitting back. He was wearing his seersucker suit again today.

"I just got interrogated."

He frowned. "What happened?"

"Are you sure you have time for this?"

Max waved to the chair in front of his desk, and Slater dropped into it, and told him about Chila and the insurance regulators.

"Do you think they'll actually try to mess things up for you with Cudahy Mutual?"

"I doubt it," Slater said. "I'm thinking it was an empty threat. A lame-ass attempt to gain leverage over me. Della probably wouldn't even care if they brought it to her."

Max nodded. "DOI is probably obligated to look into it. They're just throwing stuff at the wall to see what sticks, to see if they can get a reaction from you. Confirmation, maybe, or for you to turn on Chila."

"Do you remember Silvana Lee?"

"How could I forget? The grifter in true vermillion."

"That guy who ran the clothing company told me a story about driving through the desert. He'd just graduated college in the East and was moving back to LA. He came to a road junction, and one of those green highway signs pointed left to some distant town, and right to some other town. He realized he could go either way. He said he sat there for a while, and thought about it, just soaking up the limitless possibilities. The idea that he could do anything next."

"That's a great feeling," Max said. "Knowing you have options."

"So why did Chila choose to rat me out? It's like she turned the wrong way."

"It seems to me it would sabotage her bunco game. You easily could have pointed the finger back at her."

"She knows I wouldn't do that."

"Even so, I would think it reduces her chances of getting the guy's money."

"It was a long shot anyway," Slater said. "I don't actually know what her plan was. I assume it would be pretty reliant on Woody being dumb."

"Maybe she's doing this to sow confusion, so she can get on with the grift without you interfering."

"That would only work if she found Woody without my help." He threw up his hands. "Maybe she was worried I was going to turn her in, so she beat me to the punch to protect herself."

"Chila sounds like a real bearcat."

"I know I should be angry," Slater said, "but it hasn't hit me yet. I'm not thinking rationally these days."

"Because of your romance?" Max said.

"Emotionally it's weird. I'm not used to it. It feels like standing in the middle of a forest fire. There are flames all around, and searing heat, and embers flying everywhere."

"I like Pike a lot. He seems like a solid person."

"I think he's got some pheromone imbalance," Slater said. "It's why I'm so into him. He's emitting intoxicating chemicals that mess up my brain."

"Or you're just really into him." Max chuckled and sat back, making a wide gesture. "It happens."

"You know how it is when it's new, and everything's still good?"

"Oh, yeah. I got through that eventually with Vanessa. It probably took half a year."

"She's way too good for you."

"I know that better than anybody," Max said. "I've told her that repeatedly. I think it's why I have trouble trusting her. I'm always asking myself, why is she really with me?"

"Do you think Pike is too good for me?"

"I don't know him well enough," Max said. "He's a lawman, and if he keeps his nose clean, that could be a speed bump for guys like us."

"He seems like he's pretty much by the book."

Max sat up. "So are you going to let it drop? The thing with Chila."

"Obviously I have to go after her."

"Or you could let it drop."

Slater slowly shook his head. "You know that saying: if you can't get justice, you can get revenge."

"There's also a saying that seeking revenge is like digging two graves, and one of them is for your damn self."

"Nobody's going to get planted," Slater said. "I'm not that crazy."

"At least hang on to the thing about being calm. It'll go better if you're mostly rational."

"Even though you sound like all the shrinks Doris sent me to in middle school," he said, raising his eyebrows, "that actually sounds right."

TWENTY

WHEN SLATER PULLED THE Thunderbird into his garage, he felt drained. But there was still some daylight left, and he pulled down a leaf rake from the wall rack, and grabbed a big black garbage bag.

Upstairs, just past the kitchen counters, a door led out onto a landing and a narrow flight of metal stairs up to the roof. Slater trudged up and stepped over the low wall that surrounded it. The building was new enough that the flat roof conformed to the current building code, surfaced in white to reflect the heat.

The idiot gentrifiers who'd built the place had never cleaned up the leaves, and big piles of them had blown into the front corners, blocking the drains. Eventually they'd start making soil, and that would retain water, and the water would come through. Flat roofs were notorious for leaks.

Working carefully so as not to scratch the surface material, he started raking them up.

Lots of these were laurel leaves, he saw. Those were shed in late winter and spring. Some of it was palm detritus, the sturdy fronds that came loose in any stiff breeze. Eventually he had it all loaded into the bag. In the looming twilight he made sure the drains were clear, and looked around the roof, satisfied with his work. He carried the bag down to the kitchen, and eyed the vases of flowers in the big room. They'd look OK for another day or two, but this bag was only half full. He spent a minute grabbing the aging arrangements and stuffing them in with the leaves, then carried the bag down and dumped it in the green bin.

Once he'd washed up, back upstairs, the room looked empty without all the flora. The gray of twilight descending made it feel even more barren. Slater stretched out on the sofa. He needed to think things through, plan how to handle Chila, and figure out what to do about Woody's money. He wondered whether Woody had had time to cool off. He sent him a text:

> We need to talk. There's more going on than you know. Get over yourself and call me.

Looking through the last few messages, he tapped on the conversation labeled "Reddy Kilowatt" and texted Pike:

> I can taste your mouth right now. I want to suck your fingers. I want you inside me.

Setting his phone facedown on his chest, he picked it up a moment later when it buzzed with Pike's reply. It was a GIF of a dachshund slowly nodding its head, superimposed with the word SOON.

Slater chuckled and muttered, "Idiot."

He dozed for a while, and when he woke saw that it was fully dark out now. Under his booze rules, that was the third green light: the day was over, he wasn't going to work anymore, and he was in for the night. Rising, he went to the kitchen and poured his ration into a tumbler, plus an extra finger or so as a premium. He'd been interrogated today—he deserved it.

Taking a gulp, he closed his eyes to savor the heady bourbon, and relished the burn in his throat. Before he'd made it back to the sofa, the door-bell rang, startling him mid-sip, and he coughed. Who the hell was that? Setting the tumbler on the kitchen counter, he hustled down the stairs and pulled open the door.

Woody stood there, wearing pink shorts and a billowy white shirt, his expression somber.

"Why aren't you at work?" Slater said.

"Musicians don't work Mondays. It's our night off."

"Who knew."

Woody frowned. "Are you going to let me come in?"

"Are you going to behave?" Slater said. "You know that if you take a poke at me, it's not going to end well for you."

"I'm not going to do that." He heaved a sigh.

"We both know I can't make you do anything."

"Are you armed?"

"What?" He scowled. "Of course not."

Slater moved aside to let him in, eyeing his belt. Those shorts were pretty snug, and there was no sign of a weapon under them.

As Woody stepped past, he said, "You smell like a bar. Are you drinking?"

"I was actually just getting started."

When they got upstairs, Woody flicked on the room lights, then walked over to the sofa.

"No more flowers," he said.

"Nothing lasts forever." On the way by, Slater retrieved his tumbler from the kitchen counter, and gestured with it as he stepped over. "Want a taste?"

"No," Woody said flatly.

"Suit yourself." Slater took the chair facing him and set the tumbler aside. He needed to focus, and he could already feel the warmth of that first slug of bourbon.

"I got a call from my friend Il Capitano today. He asked me if I knew a Mexican insurance guy who had a short temper and wore jeans on the hottest day of the year."

"I'm not Mexican."

"He said you beat the shit out of him."

Slater chuckled. "If I'd beaten the shit out of him, he wouldn't be gossiping on the phone, he'd be on a ventilator in a coma. Ask him to photograph his injuries. He won't because there aren't any."

"Why are you stalking me?" Woody demanded, raising his voice.

"I'm not." He frowned. "Not anymore. Before we met, I did some digging into your background. I know you changed your name."

He folded his arms. "OK. That's not really a secret."

"But it's also not information that's readily available. The insurance companies and Lindsay Nguyen didn't know."

"Who the fuck is Lindsay Nguyen?" Woody shouted.

"Settle down. We'll get to that. Do you know anyone who'd have named you as beneficiary on a life insurance policy? Using your old name."

"No," he said flatly. "Why were you looking into my background, and hassling my business associates?"

"If you mean Les James," Slater said, "I talked to her for a hot minute before she threw me out of her place. Your name was never mentioned."

"You asked Il Capitano about me."

"That guy is a dud. Don't you think he's more of a Brighella than a Capitano? I think his business model is basically a swindle. You'd be wise to steer clear of him."

"Slater—focus." Woody sat up. "What insurance policy are you talking about?"

"You know that research is part of my job, right?"

Something flickered in Woody's eyes, and his brow furrowed.

"Come to think of it, I remember something about life insurance. My father worked for this management company. They had a policy on him. I think I was supposed to be the beneficiary."

"When was this?"

"A long time ago. I was still in middle school, or maybe high school. My dad had a big job. But I suppose you knew that already."

"I know his surname was Hassan."

"I'm not sure exactly what my father did for them, but he was gone a lot. I was told the company wanted to help me out in case he died."

"That's called dead peasant insurance."

Woody scowled. "My parents weren't peasants. They actually had a little money."

"I'm not judging them," Slater said. "That's the industry term for that kind of policy. The company wanted to protect itself from liability. So that you or your mother wouldn't go after them with a lawsuit."

"Setting up that kind of policy means I couldn't sue them?"

"Somebody else can't sign away your right to undertake legal action," Slater said, "but if you get an insurance payout, it's less likely you'd want to sue them. Also a judge might say, 'Well, you already got some dough,' and reject the suit, or at least reduce the amount of any award. On average it saves them money."

"Freaking vampires. Long live corporate America."

"When your father died, that policy must have paid out. The insurance company couldn't find Woodrow Hassan. When they gave up, the money was put in trust with the state controller. Lindsay Nguyen."

Woody's brow furrowed. "That's what all this is about? You skulking around Greenleaf, and hitting on me in a thrift store, and getting me into your bed?"

"I didn't exactly have to twist your arm for that part, you big dick hound." Slater gestured helplessly. "I needed to make sure you were the guy. That you weren't running some kind of scheme to get somebody else's payout. I thought maybe you and Il Capitano were collaborating on a badger game. That happens a lot in the entertainment business."

Woody scoffed. "So how do I get the dough?"

"I know a woman who can advise you. My lawyer. She'll explain it."

"Lawyers, man." Woody shook his head. "Is she going to charge me more than what I'm owed? How much money is it, anyway?"

"She can get into all that with you. She's not going to rip you off. If you don't like her, you can find your own lawyer."

Woody threw up his hands. "I can't say that I completely trust you, but I know you well enough to know you wouldn't work with a lawyer who'd scam you."

"Let me text her," Slater said, and pulled out his phone, and thumb-typed a note to O'Dowd:

> Do you have time for a consult tomorrow? It's a simple job.

As he tucked his phone away, Woody spoke. "So you want to know why I changed my name."

"Personally, I don't really care. It's a detail."

"It mattered enough that you dug it up."

Slater stifled a sigh and reached for his tumbler. "Why did you change your name, Woody?"

"Maybe I married a guy named Newkirk, and I wanted to take his name."

"Maybe?" He frowned. "You're not sure whether you got married?"

"Maybe people always thought I was Muslim," Woody said, his gaze level, "and I got sick of it, so I picked a bland Anglo name."

"Are you Muslim?"

"Maybe my parents got in some trouble, and I wanted to distance myself from them."

"People make mistakes." Slater gestured with his tumbler. "People do bad things. I certainly do. You saw the frayed edges of that part of me on Saturday night at Greenleaf. We all have secrets, and we all lie, and we all do fucking stupid things. But nobody is beyond redemption."

"My parents are. They're both dead."

"I guess that's about as much distance as you can get."

Woody looked away. "You're right. It's not your business, or anybody else's."

"The only person in all this who has a legitimate reason to ask questions about your identity is Lindsay Nguyen."

He rose. "I should go. You'll let me know about your lawyer?"

"I'm sure she'll call me in the morning. Plan on seeing her tomorrow."

"Where's her office?"

"Westwood. I'll go with you to make the intro-duction." Slater set aside his tumbler and stood up. "You can stay if you want. I have a warm bed."

"And you call me a dick hound." Woody scoffed. "You're a total addict, you know that? We just hooked up this afternoon."

"I remember. We could just sleep."

"Like that would happen," he said flatly.

"Yeah, I guess that is basically the old bait-and-switch. It was worth a shot."

"Save it for Reddy Kilowatt."

Woody strode over to the stairs, and Slater lis-tened as he descended, and then heard the front door close. Slamming what was left in his tumbler, he went back to the kitchen and poured another couple of fingers.

Once he'd killed the lights, he went to the sofa, and turned on the radio, and stretched out in the dark. This station was usually pretty dead-ass on weeknights, but they were playing decent house music, and he sank into it.

Woody was right, he knew. He needed to focus on Pike, and keep his dick in his pants until they were together. Right now he needed to round out his plan for Chila. Thinking about it, the ideas that coalesced got more elaborate as the warmth of the amber elixir suffused his mind. But he knew he needed to be sober to think it through clearly, and he pushed it away, and embraced sweet oblivion.

TWENTY-ONE

A RINGING PHONE, SLATER REALIZED, swimming up to consciousness. Daylight streamed in the window. He grabbed it off the nightstand and answered, "Ibáñez."

"Did I wake you?" It was O'Dowd's voice.

"I'm up." He tried to enunciate clearly even though his tongue felt thick and his mouth was dry. "I'm just eating some peanut butter."

"I believe that like I believe your expense reports," she said. "You owe me one of those, by the way."

"I'm actually working on it as we speak. Listen, do you have time for me today? I want to bring a client over to talk to you."

"I saw your text. What kind of client?"

Slater sat up, and rubbed his eyes, and explained the situation with Woody. Once he'd ended the call, he sent Woody a text:

My lawyer can meet you today.

Slater was up and dressed and slurping steaming java when the doorbell rang. He trotted down to open the door and found Woody, wearing a blue dress shirt and dark trousers.

"The tired canary."

Woody frowned. "What?"

"You look sleepy."

"It's early. I work nights, remember?"

"We don't have to leave for a while," Slater said. "Do you want some joe?"

"Hit me."

They climbed up to the kitchen, and Slater poured a cup for him from the carafe.

"Can we sit outside for a minute?" Woody said. "I feel like the daylight will help me wake up. I'm not a morning person."

Slater followed him out onto the deck. It was hot out, but the morning sun felt good.

"I've been thinking about your story," Woody said, sipping his coffee and then setting the mug on the table.

"It's not a story, toots. It's cold hard facts. The immutable and unwavering truth. The golden threads that stitch this world together."

"You didn't explain how it all started. How did you know Woody Hassan had a payout languishing at the state controller's office?"

"I'm in insurance," Slater said. "It's my job."

"So someone is paying you to track down people like me? The fact that the insurance company gave it to the state implies that they've washed their hands of it."

"Nobody's paying me. I learned about it in the course of my duties."

Woody eyed him for a moment. "Now you sound like a politician." He reached for his mug. "How do you know this lawyer?"

"Her name is O'Dowd. She's also an accountant and does the books for my business. She's canny—doesn't ask too many questions, gets results fast, and knows how to weasel out of tight spots." Slater's phone buzzed, and he pulled it out. "Speak of the devil."

"Can you come over a little earlier?" O'Dowd said when he picked up. "My morning opened up, and it's kind of messed up the rest of my day."

"We can be there in about forty."

"Great. I haven't seen you in so long, I'm not sure I'll even recognize you."

"I'll be wearing a white gardenia," he said flatly, and ended the call.

Woody raised his eyebrows. "Are you actually going to wear a flower?"

"Gardenias are done for the season." He waggled his phone. "I hear from her all the time. It's basically harassment. 'I need this,' 'I need that.' Income reports, expense reports, schedule C. *Ksh, ksh*." He mimed a kovac, slapping the air left and right. "But we don't meet very often. She just said she doesn't remember what I look like. I might have to bust up her office. That would be memorable."

Woody frowned. "You should probably just

wear the gardenia. And maybe lay off the caffeine."

"We should go." He drained his mug and rose. "You can drive."

Slater locked the door on the way out, and they climbed into the yellow Bronco.

"I love this car," Slater said. "It's a total dick magnet."

Woody laughed as he pulled into the street. "What's the best way?"

Checking the navigation app on his phone, he directed him onto the 10. Once they were on the streets of Westwood, he pointed out the parking under O'Dowd's building.

The elevators from the garage were blocked off with white-painted construction plywood, and arrows pointed the way toward the side street. They walked through a narrow tunnel of more plywood and emerged on Wilshire. Slater looked around to get his bearings, then gestured to the building's main entrance.

"This kind of office tower seems so corporate," Woody said, raising his voice over the noise of the traffic.

"O'Dowd is a one-woman firm. She said she got cheap rent here for some reason. Maybe she does for the landlord what she does for me."

"I just don't trust lawyers."

"I get it, but you need them once in a while. You can't disconnect her work from what you do either. She's part of it, and you're part of it."

"Part of what?"

Slater waved at the cars on the boulevard and

the row of office towers that turned it into a canyon. "The game we're playing to keep all this going."

They walked into the lobby and rode up to O'Dowd's floor. Slater knocked on her door and pushed it open. It was a small office, crowded with furniture and messy with stacks of paper and file folders and thick binders, colorful sticky notes protruding from the pages like confetti. O'Dowd was in her forties, her spiky African hair held back by an orange band. She was more dressed up than he'd ever seen her, in a somber jacket, gold jewelry gleaming at her neck. She'd probably spiffed up because she was meeting a new client.

Slater introduced them, and Woody reached across the desk to shake her hand, flashing that confident smile.

Once they were seated across from her, O'Dowd tented her fingers and eyed Woody. "Slater gave me the run-down on your situation. My assessment is that you could file a claim with the state controller yourself, but because it's such a large amount, and because of the name-change complication, it's probably wise to get my help."

Woody glanced sidelong at Slater and frowned. "That seems gossipy."

"Look at me," O'Dowd said, her tone intent. "I'm in your corner here. Slater and I have a legally privileged relationship. That covers you too. It means I can't tell anyone else anything about your affairs."

"What do you mean by 'a large amount'?" Woody said.

Her eyebrows rose. "I looked it up myself. The payout held for Woodrow Hassan is north of three million dollars."

"Are you kidding me?"

"I'm serious as a heart attack, brother."

He stared at her for a moment, then eyed Slater. "I see now why you wanted to call in a lawyer."

"It's your money, no matter what," O'Dowd said. "But going after it in the right way will save you a lot of pain."

"What's it going to cost me?"

"For my time?" O'Dowd said. "If there aren't any complications, let's say three grand. I don't see any reason we'd have to file a suit, but if we do, it'll be more."

Slater stood up. "If you've got it from here, I'm going to hit the bricks."

"Dude," Woody said. "It's three million clams."

"Mazel tov."

He leaned over and slapped Slater's thigh with the back of his hand. "I just … I'm grateful that you found this."

"Like the woman said, it's your dough." Slater shrugged. "I'm sure whatever that corporation did to your father, it's not even close to fair compensation."

He walked out, and down to the street, and headed toward the metro. The blazing sun was high in the sky, and by the time he was on the platform, he was feeling the heat, and pushed the sweat through his hair with a hand.

As he waited for the train, he scrolled through

his contacts, and eventually found it: Finn, a film industry guy he'd hooked up with once. Slater dialed, glad that he picked up.

"Hey, hot stuff. It's been a minute."

"You do special effects, correct?" Slater said. "I need to acquire some fake blood."

"I can get you some of that. You need a bottle of it? What for? Halloween is months away."

"Aren't there little packets that actors use to make it look like they've been wounded?"

"I can get those too."

"Can it be today?"

"I'm at the theater," Finn said. "I know there's some of those here."

Slater had no idea the guy worked at a theater. "Where's that, exactly?" he said, watching the train slow as it approached.

"In Sierra Madre." He rattled off the address. "I'll be here all day."

As he stepped onto the train, he ended the call and thumb-typed the address into a note. If he could get the props today, there was no reason to delay meeting Chila. He found a seat and dialed her number. When she answered, her tone was guarded.

"Hey, Slater. What's up?"

"I've got good news. I think I might have found the guy. You'll have to decide whether it's really him."

"I wasn't sure you were going to play along."

She didn't know the insurance regulators had already talked to him, Slater realized.

"Why wouldn't I play along?" he said. "We made a deal."

"So where is he?"

"I'm not going to tell you on the phone. You'll try to cut me out. We'll meet, and I'll give you the details, and we'll discuss my role in the next phase."

"Are you at your office?" Chila said.

"I've got some stuff to do. There's a brewpub on Spring. Meet me there at 6:30."

"Can it be a little earlier?"

"No way," he said. "That's when I'm available. Unless you want to postpone a couple days."

"I'll make it work," she said quickly.

"Don't be late, or I'll bail."

Slater ended the call. It had to be 6:30—the cops' shift change was at 6, and he needed them to be there. A few uniforms were usually hanging around that place, as it was cheap and not far from police headquarters.

Public transit was slow but it allowed for more mental bandwidth than driving. He used the time to think through his plan for Chila, and shore up the soft points, and consider the contingencies.

Downtown, he climbed out of the ground and walked to Hill Street, and waited for the bus to take him to his neighborhood. These routes had been the same his whole life, he thought idly, once he was aboard and staring out the window as the 4 rolled up Sunset Boulevard. The same numbers plying the same streets as when he'd been in elementary school, and probably long before that. Architecture in LA was like a sandbox, with structures both prominent and mundane routinely erected and erased and replaced with the next thing. But they didn't move the streets around very often.

Once he was upstairs, he stretched out on his bed to chill for a minute, not bothering to take off his boots, and not quite drifting off. He checked the clock on his phone. It was time to set things in motion.

Rising, he stretched, and went down to the garage, backing the Thunderbird into the street. Sierra Madre was way east, a suburb of a suburb, but at least the whole trip was on freeways.

Eventually he pulled up at the address Finn had given him, a long low 1960s building. It had to be a conversion. Before it was a theater it might have been an office, or a medical building. The door was locked when he tried it, so he pressed the adjacent bell.

Finn appeared inside the glass, and beamed at the sight of him. Despite his name he had an indigenous look, in his cheekbones and his eyes, and his dark hair was cropped short. He was wearing light summery trousers, and his tropical shirt, in bright greens and blues, looked vintage.

Unlocking the door, Finn waved him in. "You look great."

"Back at you," Slater said. "I didn't know this was where you worked."

"Mostly everyone volunteers. There's so much down time between film projects. Even the big names in the industry need other stuff to do."

Slater glanced around the lobby. It was quiet

and empty. "Just you today?"

"There might be some other people wandering around. Come on."

Slater followed him into a stairwell, then a hallway, and into a space with COSTUMES AND PROPS written on the door. Racks of clothing filled one side of the big room, several rows deep and climbing up the wall, like in a shop. Along another wall was wire shelving with an array of junk—wood and metal parts, cardboard boxes, plastic tubs.

Stepping sideways along the shelves, sometimes stooping to read the labels on the boxes lower down, Finn scanned the collection until eventually he pulled out a tub. He set it on the worktable in the middle of the room and pulled off the lid, then handed Slater a little packet, smaller than his palm. Made of a soft stretchy material, it was translucent, its contents fluid and dark red.

"Careful with that," Finn said. "It'll burst in your hands."

"It doesn't look like a lot of volume."

"Trust me, it's plenty. When it breaks it's very dramatic. What exactly are you planning to do with it?"

"I can't get into detail, but I need to fake an injury. It has to look real. Not like a cartoon. I need to fool someone up close."

"This stuff is the right color, and the right viscosity," Finn said. "The difference is that real blood dries quickly and gets darker. This won't do that. But at first glance, for a few minutes, it'll be convincing."

Slater studied the little pouch. "How does it work?"

"You just slap it or squeeze it. The end with the blue mark is where it'll break. You'll have blood all over. If you're going to put it under your shirt, make a little hole in the fabric first so that it really oozes. It works better if you tape the pouch to the inside of the garment, not to your skin."

"Can I put it in my mouth?"

"That type is meant to go under your clothes." Finn dug in the tub and produced another little pouch, handing it to him. "This one fits in your cheek."

It was oval in shape, with a protrusion in the middle the size of a nipple.

"Tuck it in your cheek and bite on the bumpy part. You'll be spewing blood." Finn chuckled. "It's actually pretty shocking to see it happen."

"Will it show on my face," Slater said, "or make me sound different?"

"Try it out." Fin led him over to a mirror, on the wall near the door, that stretched floor to ceiling. "It won't break unless you bite it."

Standing in front of the mirror, Slater tucked the packet into his cheek.

"It's shaped to fit in there and be invisible."

"It makes my face look a little puffy on that side," Slater said. It felt like his words were slightly muffled too, although the tone of his voice hadn't changed.

"Considering how much product is in there, it's very well hidden."

"Is it toxic if I swallow it?"

"It's designed for that eventuality," Finn said. "It's mostly corn syrup, so it's edible. And unlike lots of things you've had in your mouth, it's sterile."

Slater chuckled and pulled it out, gently blotting the saliva on his pants. "I'll need some of both."

"Are two of the mouth ones enough?" Finn said, stepping back to the work table.

"Give me four, so I can practice. Does it have a stale date?"

"If it gets lumpy, just squish it a little to mix it up again." He went over to the wire shelves, and returned with a brown paper lunch bag, and tucked several of the pouches into it.

"What do I owe you for this?"

Finn grinned. "You don't have to pay me."

"A donation to the theater, then."

"We have angels that take care of that. Not literally mythological beings that descend from the sky to deliver cash, but rich folks who need a tax deduction. People with more money than you'll see in your whole lifetime."

TWENTY-TWO

"THERE'S ANOTHER THING," SLATER said. "I need to take a dive, and it needs to look real. You're in the theater—do you have a minute to show me how?"

"I haven't really been on the stage recently," Finn said, raising his eyebrows. "I'm behind the scenes these days."

"But you know how to do it."

"I suppose my skills won't have faded. Will you be standing, or sitting down?"

"In a chair."

Finn nodded. "Come." He stepped toward the door, and tapped a folding chair that was leaning against the wall. "Bring this."

Once Slater had carried it into the hall, Finn pulled the door closed and walked the opposite way from the lobby. After a couple of turns, he stopped at a set of industrial electric switches on the wall and flipped several of them on. Stage lighting, Slater realized. Behind him spotlights came on, high above, illuminating the stage. They walked out under them, into the big airy space, and Finn took the chair and folded it open.

There were seats on three sides, Slater saw, peering into the gloom, all facing the stage. It was an odd experience, to see such an expansive hall completely lifeless apart from the pair of them.

"What's the capacity of this place?"

"About four fifty," Finn said. "We've been rehearsing an athletic piece, so the floor cover is soft. It's perfect to practice falling down."

Slater pressed it with the toe of his boot. It was spongy like a playground surface. Facing the hall, Finn sat bolt upright in the chair, and put his hands on his knees.

"Take a swing at me." He held up a palm. "You know I mean a stage swing."

Slater grinned and dropped to one knee in front of him, then mimed a slap. As his palm touched Finn's cheek, his head snapped away, and he tumbled to the floor, and rolled onto his side. Hopping to his feet a moment later, he beamed.

"Damn, you're good," Slater said. "That totally looked real."

"Let me show you again."

Finn ran through it, and watching closely, Slater saw that he started to fall at the same moment he turned his head.

"Your turn," Finn said, on his feet again.

Slater sat in the chair, and Finn spent a few

minutes teaching him how to snap his head side-ways.

"When you hit ninety degrees, your torso nat-urally follows the twist. Push with your left leg." Finn tapped his knee. "That'll make it look like the blow knocked you bodily out of the chair."

They ran through it again, and Slater hit the floor several more times. It wasn't painless, despite the spongy surface, and he massaged his shoulder as he stood up.

"Does it look convincing?" Slater said.

"No one is likely to be watching you closely, correct? It'll be convincing to anyone who sees it in the periphery. But don't ham it up too much."

"What does that mean?"

"Don't exaggerate your movements. You were struck in the face, so your legs don't need to be spas-ming like you're having a seizure. Keep it natural."

Slater nodded. It was good advice.

"The spectators will be nearby?" Finn said.

"That's the plan."

"When you hit the deck, you should also cover your face. That's what other people are looking at. If you hide your face, it makes you look more injured." He whirled a finger in the air. "Once more, and cover your face."

Finn mimed the slap, and Slater's head snapped, and he pushed off with his leg. Tumbling onto his side, he curled up, covering his face with his hands.

"You're a natural."

Slater stood up and rolled his neck. "I think I got it."

"So—maybe we can get together again," Finn said, picking up the chair and folding it closed. "I remember we had fun."

"That was fun," Slater said as he scooped up the little paper bag. "But I'm kind of getting involved with someone. I need to focus on that."

"I won't say I'm not disappointed."

"Hearing myself say it, I sound so square and boring."

Finn shrugged. "He's a lucky man."

They walked off the stage, and Finn killed the lights, then led the way to the lobby.

"Good luck with whatever it is you're up to," Finn said, unlocking the door for him.

Once he was back at his house, Slater carried the paper bag up to his bedroom, and pulled off his boots, and stripped off his clothes. Digging out one of the mouth pouches, he tucked it into his cheek. It wasn't that uncomfortable, but he certainly wouldn't forget it was there.

Tucking one of the other pouches into his hand, he stepped into the shower, but then realized he needed to see himself. Back in the bedroom, he grabbed the floor mirror and carried it into the bathroom, and set it facing the glass wall of the shower stall. Stepping in again, he faced the mirror, and took a deep breath. The pouch in his hand was small enough that he could palm it, and it would stay unseen. With his other hand he slapped his cheek, at the same time biting down on the pouch's little nub.

His mouth instantly filled with sweet thick

liquid. It was viscous, a little like thin oil. His instinct was to swallow it, but he spit it out instead, startled at the sight of a flood of bright red on his chin, then running down his neck.

Finn was right—this was plenty of blood. There was something visceral about seeing it, like it tapped a deep part of his brain and raised an alarm.

He slapped the other pouch hard onto his shoulder. The force of the blow broke it open, and another dramatic red blotch dribbled down over his pec. There was so much blood now it looked like a massacre. He bared his teeth, oozing with that alarming shade of red. It was a gruesome sight. Slater had to laugh. This was going to work great.

Turning on the water, he spat out the pouch and started to rinse the stuff off. Thick but not really oily, it washed away easily.

Once he'd toweled off, he went to get dressed, in a white T-shirt and an old pair of jeans that he didn't mind getting trashed. One of each of the pouches would be plenty, he decided, and down in the garage he put the others in a drawer on his tool bench. He found a quilted moving blanket and folded it over the driver's seat of the Thunderbird. The fake blood would get all over his clothes, but he didn't need to transfer it to his car too.

Backing into the street, he waited for the garage door to roll down, then drove to his office. The parking lot was emptying out at this time of day, the attendants long gone, and he parked in a stall near the street. This wasn't really close to the pub, but he wanted to come by here afterward to clean up.

He walked the few minutes to the Civic Center, assuming a rapid stride, even though it was still plenty hot out. He wanted to burn off some of the adrenaline he felt thrumming in his body. Was Chila left-handed or right-handed? He tried to remember as he walked. Most people were righties, and when she'd punched him, she'd hit his left shoulder. But then she'd cuffed her son with her left.

A block before he got to the pub, he tucked the oval pouch into his cheek and got it positioned. It wasn't uncomfortable, but it was hard to ignore. He palmed the other pouch. Hopefully he could keep it hidden. Crumpling the paper bag, he tossed it into a street can.

Walking up on the pub, he saw a familiar face: Etta. She was standing on the sidewalk next to a lanky woman with a mane of dark hair. Her girl-friend, Safiya. They'd paused because they'd spotted him approaching. Etta greeted him with a smile, and Safiya scowled, not even attempting to mask her hostility. He knew she thought Etta's gig work for Slater and Max took up too much of her time.

"What are you doing here?" Slater said.

"We were downtown, and getting hangry," Etta said. "I'm surprised you're going to eat at this place. It's kind of meaty."

"Can we go somewhere else?" Safiya said. "I really don't want to hang out with him."

"The feeling is mutual, sister," Slater said flatly, and to Etta, "I'm running an op. I have to be alone."

Her eyebrows shot up. "In the brewpub? I want to watch."

"I really wish you wouldn't. There's another place just like this over on Main, a couple blocks down. Go eat your animals over there."

"I won't get in the way," Etta said. "I won't even look at you."

Slater huffed, and stepped closer, and lowered his voice. "It's going to be messy. No matter what happens, you don't know who I am. Don't come near me. It might look like I need your help, but I don't."

"Got it. It's a covert op."

"Don't tell anyone my name, no matter who asks. Cops or otherwise. You don't know me." He jabbed a finger at Safiya. "That goes double for you."

Safiya recoiled. "Fine with me. Can we make it permanent?"

"We'll be as unobtrusive as the wallpaper," Etta said.

He took a breath and glanced around at the street. "Are you around tomorrow? I need to paint my bedroom."

"I'm not going to help you paint your house," Etta said.

"I'll do the painting. I just need help picking a color."

"She's not your decorator," Safiya said, and frowned.

"You should see my office. It's like time-traveling to 1930. The place looks like a million bucks, and she did the whole shebang for two grand."

"Paint chips aren't as exciting as a covert op," Etta said, "but sure, I can come by."

"Don't look at me in there," he said intently, and then walked inside.

It was interesting that they hadn't noticed the blood packet. Maybe it didn't puff out his cheek as much as it felt like it did. They also hadn't commented on his speech, even though to him it felt altered.

There was no host here, as the place was too casual for that. He looked around for a moment. The bar was farther back on the left, and on the right were the booths. One of them was currently hosting a trio of cops, just as he'd hoped. They were still in uniform, coming off shift.

Between them and the bar was a short wall with a row of tables along a bench. The perfect setup would be to sit at the end of the bench, at the last table. Next to it was a patch of open floor. Sitting there, he wouldn't be facing the cops directly, but he'd be within their view, and close to the entrance if he needed to bolt. Half the tables were empty, but the one he wanted was occupied, by a pasty chubby guy sitting alone, gazing at his phone, an empty beer glass in front of him.

Slater palmed a twenty, fumbling with it as he carefully shifted the little red pouch to his other hand. He stepped up to the guy and flashed the bill.

"I want to sit here," Slater said. "My friend President Jackson would like to assist you in moving somewhere else."

"Is this your regular table or something?" he said.

"What do you care? It's free money."

"You know, Jackson evicted the tribes of the Southeast and made them walk to Oklahoma. It was a terrible way to steal the land from people. Imagine being displaced like that. This country has a lot to answer for."

"I am not taking consciousness-raising history lessons from an entitled white guy," Slater said intently. "Twenty bucks, take it or leave it."

"Show me the cash."

He shifted sideways to block the view from the cops' booth with his body, and set the twenty on the table, partly visible under his hand. The guy grabbed it, but Slater didn't let go.

"On your feet first, brother."

He scowled but got up, and Slater released the bill.

"Thank you, sir," he said, pocketing it as he walked out the door to the street.

"Dick," Slater muttered, and took his seat on the bench. He was probably about to leave anyway.

He moved the guy's empty beer glass onto the next table and looked around. Safiya and Etta had sat farther away, two booths down from the cops. Both of them were sitting on the same side, facing this way. They wanted to see what he was up to. At least neither of them were eyeballing him.

The server stepped up, a woman with short brown hair and freckles.

"What'll it be, hon?"

"A small of the lightest lager on tap."

She nodded and walked away. Chila should be

here by now. He gently probed the pouch with his tongue. Hopefully it wasn't going to melt in his saliva.

A minute later the server set down his beer, and he handed her a twenty.

"I'm expecting someone," Slater said. "She's on a separate check."

"I'll bring your change."

"I don't need change."

"Thanks," she said, and smiled as she walked away.

Glancing over at the booth with the cops, he saw there was a half-eaten plate of nachos on their table. They'd be here for a little while at least.

TWENTY-THREE

When Chila walked in, Slater's heart started to pound. He waved at her and forced a smile, trying not to disturb the packet in his cheek.

As she sat across from him, hanging her bag on the back of her chair, she studied his face, her brow furrowing. She still didn't know that he knew she'd ratted him out to the insurance regulators. But that's definitely what she was thinking about.

The server quickly stepped over and eyed Chila. Overtipping her had brought the desired effect: her immediate attention, to reinforce in her mind that Slater had already paid his tab.

"What can I get you?" she said.

"Just a beer." Chila gestured to Slater's glass. "The same as what he's having."

Once she was gone, Chila leaned toward him. "I can't believe you found Woodrow Hassan. Where is he?"

"San Diego, believe it or not," Slater said.

"What's your angle, exactly? You want to drive down there and meet him together? We should get our story straight. But I'll do the talking."

He slowly shook his head. "That's not going to happen, Chila. The three mil is all mine. I'm going to cut you out."

"You can't." She frowned. "You don't know what you're doing. This is my thing. I did all the work."

"You shouldn't have fucked with me."

"I did no such thing. I offered to bring you in on this. I didn't have to do that." She was getting flushed, her cheeks hot. "You won't get anywhere with Hassan on your own. I've got a whole plan mapped out. You need me, or you won't get anything."

"I'm willing to take that risk." Slater gestured vaguely. "It's not really your fault. It's just the way you do things. I don't think you have what it takes to pull it off."

"What are you talking about?" she demanded, raising her voice.

"Your limited intelligence. It's not a personal failing. It's just the hand you were dealt."

"I'm not stupid," she snapped.

"I'm sure you believe that. Stupid people usually do. But when you invited me into your place—"

"You broke into my place."

"That's a lie," Slater said flatly. He picked up his beer glass, and took a sip, and set it down at the left edge of the table. "Anyway, I saw how you lived."

He could see her chest heaving.

"What does that have to do with anything?" she demanded.

"I felt so bad for Eddy, living in that dump. He's at the age where he'll be figuring out that life doesn't have to be that tragic. You need to face it, Chila. You're trash. You know it, and I know it, and everyone in this pub knows it." He raised his eyebrows and spoke louder. "Trash."

Slater was sure she'd do it eventually, but he almost wasn't ready for it. Lightning fast, Chila rose slightly from her chair as she wound up, and slapped him hard across the face.

His head snapped, and he tumbled off the bench onto the floor. It was concrete, and he landed a lot harder than on the practice stage at Finn's theater. On the way down he bit on the pouch, and instantly had a cloying sweet taste on his tongue. Spewing out the liquid, he rolled on his side, and slapped the pouch in his hand onto the side of his head as he moved to cover his face. He felt it pop, and then warm liquid oozing into his hair. The stuff should be all over him now.

The empty packet—he hadn't thought about what to do with it. Clawing at the collar of his T-shirt, he tucked it inside. The one in his mouth was going to have to stay there for now.

He pulled his knees up into the fetal position, and peered through his bloodied hands. Chila was on her feet, staring at him, eyes wide, mouth agape. Several other people were on their feet now too, including a couple of the cops.

"Don't hit me again, Isidra, please," Slater shouted, still shielding his face. "Leave me alone."

One of the cops squatted beside him. "Sir, you're injured. Try to stay calm."

Slater scooted backward and waved a hand. "Keep her away from me."

The other cop was standing next to Chila, eyeing Slater, his brow furrowed. "What did you hit him with?"

"My hand," Chila said.

"Does she have a broken beer glass?" Slater said.

"That's it." The cop grabbed Chila's arm and pulled her toward the entrance.

"I hardly touched him," Chila shouted.

Once she'd been hauled out, Slater sat up.

"Just relax," the cop said.

"Could you step back a little?" he said. "You're making me nervous."

She rose, one hand absently on her radio, not speaking into it yet. She had that look in her eye—not quite doubt, rather that she was trying to assess him objectively, not yet ready to buy into a specific narrative.

"Where did you get cut?" she said.

"It might be my scalp. I think I bit my tongue on the way down too. I'm in a lot of pain here."

"Scalp wounds tend to bleed a lot," she said. "You don't look like you're in shock."

"I'm not. Listen—I'm going to press charges. You have to arrest her."

"Don't worry about that. I saw you go down. We got her dead to rights."

He got to his feet and staggered a few steps.

"Sir, you need to sit," she said, raising her voice.

He might be overselling it, he realized. Exactly the thing Finn told him not to do.

"I need some air," he said, and straightened up, and clutched a hand to his ear.

A chubby guy dressed all in black stepped close. "Let me help you."

Slater hadn't seen him before, but this had to be the bouncer. The management would definitely want the chaos moved outside. He grabbed Slater's upper arm, but he shrugged him off, and stepped toward the door. The bouncer leaned in and pushed it open for him.

When he got out to the street, the cop was right behind him. An ambulance was pulling up, it's light bar flickering red. Several passersby had stopped to see what the commotion was about. How did the ambulance get here so fast? He'd planned to disappear well before that happened.

Stepping out of the passenger side of the cab, a uniformed paramedic moved directly into his path, her gaze intent. Behind him, the cop spoke.

"Give him some room, people."

"Over here," the paramedic said, and took firm hold of his upper arm, and steered him to the end of the vehicle. She gestured to the rear bumper, and Slater leaned on it, bracing his palms on his thighs.

"My name is Roberta. I'm going to help you out." She set down her toolbox and squatted next to it, and flipped it open.

Chila and the uniform who'd hauled her outside

were nowhere in sight, he saw, glancing around. They must have already transported her to booking. A few yards away, among the small crowd of people standing around on the sidewalk watching the commotion, a bright light came on. A video camera, he realized, with a floodlight on it. Why was there a film crew here? The light illuminated the woman standing in front of the camera. In heavy makeup, she was wearing a sleeveless top and had a carefully coiffed blond mane. The microphone in her hand bore a TV station logo. She was getting set up to tape a news segment, adjusting her blouse and her jewelry and her hair.

"Hey, channel 6," Slater called to her. "You want to talk to me? I'll give you an exclusive."

The paramedic stood up, blocking his view, and peered at him intently. Gloved in powder-blue latex now, she reached for his scalp. Slater batted her hand away.

"I need to see the wounds, sir. What happened to your mouth?"

"I must have bit my tongue when I hit the floor," Slater said. "It really hurts. She hit my scalp. I think it's bleeding under my hair. Scalp wounds tend to bleed a lot."

"Still, it seems like a lot of blood, considering you're ambulatory."

She rubbed her fingers together and peered at the bright red on them. It must have transferred from his clothes when she'd steered him over here.

Her brow furrowed. "I don't think all of this is blood."

"I was eating pancakes," Slater said. "Maybe the perp hit me with the plate. I remember the sound of breaking crockery. It hit my head and shattered. My blood must be mixed with the pancake syrup."

"OK," she said evenly, and eyed him. "Are you still bleeding? I really need to have a look at your scalp."

"Don't worry about that, Roberta. Can you tell me if I have a concussion?"

She dutifully pulled a penlight from her breast pocket and aimed it in his eye, then the other. "I'd say you're fine. What's your name?"

"Nice try, sister. You want to send me a big fat medical bill, and enrich your private equity masters. Think about where all the money goes. They charge me five grand just to talk to you, and then they pay you minimum wage."

"I work for the city, you pinko," she said. "I need your name for my report."

Slater stood erect. "We're done, Roberta."

Stepping over to the reporter with the mike, he saw she was holding it out to one of the bystanders, the camera and its floodlight aimed at the guy.

"Hey, channel 6," Slater said. "What's your name?"

The reporter glanced at him, her eyes flicking down to his shirt. She quickly withdrew the mike from the person she was interviewing, cutting him off in mid-sentence. As she thrust it at Slater, she flipped her hair with her nails, and the camera swiveled to him, it's bright light making him wince.

"I know you know me," she said, and smiled. "I'm

on almost every night. Channel 6, your number-one local news source."

"I'm still a little dazed," Slater said, and squinted at her. "With my extensive injuries it's hard to see your face."

She scoffed. "It's Mary Louise. What happened here tonight?"

He felt the glare of the camera's light on him, and furrowed his brow, and leaned into the mike.

"She just freaked out," he said. "I've never seen anything like it. I told her I wasn't willing to do what she wanted—to act so unethically—and she hit me with something, and started punching me, and threw me on the floor." He screwed his eyes shut and bit his lower lip, then held a knuckle to his mouth, as if stifling a sob.

"You're safe now," Mary Louise said. "What's your name, sir?"

"She threw pancakes at me," Slater said, making his voice break, and wiped his cheek, careful not to smear the red stuff into his eyes. "I'm still a little traumatized."

"Is the perpetrator a business associate?"

"Her name is Isidra Suárez." He spelled her surname. "Nickname Chila. She's a failed insurance clerk. She tried to pull me into her filthy world of criminal activity, but I told her I just don't swing that way."

"What exactly did she want you to do?"

Even through the glare of the spotlight, he could see one of the cops talking to the paramedic, Roberta, standing over by the ambulance. Roberta's arms were folded, and they were both eyeing him. He knew that look—they weren't convinced.

"Mary Louise, thank you for your compassion," Slater said. "I can feel it. Right here, you know?" He thumped his chest with the top of his fist. "Everyone in the city thanks you for all the good work you do."

She preened and flipped her hair with a hand.

"I need to go get these wounds stitched up before I bleed out," he said, and walked away.

"You didn't tell us your name," Mary Louise called after him.

Slater headed up the sidewalk, away from the vehicles and the crowd.

"Sir?" It was the cop. Louder, she called, "Excuse me, sir? We need to get your statement."

This was the moment of truth. He could be going to jail tonight. In a dustup, sometimes they detained everybody involved until they figured it all out. But maybe not with a news crew watching their every move. It wasn't worth the risk of bad press, arresting someone the public would perceive as the bloodied victim of a crime.

Glancing back, he saw the cop half-heartedly jogging after him.

"Leave me alone," he shouted, and walked faster.

At the corner he glanced back. She wasn't following him now, instead just standing there watching him retreat—and talking into her radio. If she had any job experience, she'd know it was pointless to detain him for being a victim. But she was young. Maybe she was summoning a prowl car to intercept him. He took a deep breath. This had gotten more complicated than he'd planned.

At the next corner he spat the empty blood packet into the gutter and then hustled across the street against the light. A pedestrian walking toward him glanced at him, then did a double take, a look of alarm on his face.

No sign of reinforcements yet, he saw, swiveling his head around. But he'd only walked a few more paces when a prowl car turned the corner a block farther up, headed right toward him and moving slow. There were tents here, lining the sidewalk, and the viable pedestrian route was on the outside, along the parking meters. Slater stepped into the narrow space between the tents and the wall of the building and crouched down, then lay flat on the concrete. Unless they'd already spotted him, he'd be hidden from a passing vehicle.

He'd taken it too far. He saw that now. Cops and an ambulance and freaking Mary Louise. Too much fake blood. The paramedic had known it wasn't real. Now he was headed to jail himself.

The flap of the tent next to him flipped open, and a woman's face peered out.

"You can't sleep here," she said, and frowned. "This is my turf."

"I'll only be here for a minute," he hissed. "I'm trying not to get arrested."

"That's a lot of blood. Did they do that to you?"

Slater didn't answer, tapping a finger to his lips, as the prowl car's searchlight went on. It slowly panned over his head, illuminating the wall above and the woman's hunched silhouette inside the orange nylon of the tent. He flattened his cheek to the concrete, and breathed through his mouth to avoid the sharp organic tang in the air.

"Damn poh-lice," he heard someone grumble from the next tent.

The cops couldn't see him, he was sure of that. The searchlight went off, and he heard the car roll farther down the block. The woman was still watching him, not speaking. Her expression was neutral, not judging his alarming appearance, just sharing the experience. When you had next to nothing, all the pretenses got stripped away, like he'd done to the suckers on Doris's rosebushes. The ego got obliterated the way he'd hammered the bud cells. If they were lucid, dealing with homeless people sometimes felt like this, simple and raw and honest. No bullshit, no agenda.

Eventually it had been long enough. The cops had to be gone. Slater pulled out his wad of cash and handed her a twenty.

"Thanks for not ratting on me," he said.

She plucked the bill from his fingers and it disappeared. "We have to stick together," she said. "These are our streets."

He got to his feet, still crouching, and looked out over the tents. There was no prowl car, no traffic. Standing erect, Slater strode up the sidewalk. He started to breathe easier.

In the next block a guy swerved and stepped into the gutter to avoid him. He didn't need that kind of attention, someone else who might summon the cops, and he walked faster. Soon enough he was at his office building. The lobby was empty and quiet. He knew where there was a bigger restroom than the one on his floor, and he rode the elevator to six. Stepping up to the sink, he was startled by his own image in the mirror. A shocking amount of fake blood stained his shirt. The color really popped on the white fabric, and it was all over his face and his neck, still a lurid bright red. No wonder people had avoided him. Plucking paper towels from the dispenser, he cleaned off as much of it as he could.

It was all over his pants too, and eventually, when he was satisfied he wouldn't transfer any of the goop to the Thunderbird, he rode down to the street, and trotted across to the surface lot.

When he got to his house, he dumped his shirt and pants directly into the garbage in the garage, then went up and took a lengthy shower. The stuff had been in his hair so long that it was starting to dry out and get matted.

The floor mirror was still here, and he used it to make sure he'd washed it all away, twisting to look at his butt and baring his teeth. There was still red in his ear, he saw, and spent a minute washing it out.

Once he was clean, and toweled off, he felt exhausted. It hadn't been a lot of physical labor but it was a serious adrenaline rush. He trudged upstairs to the kitchen, still naked. Why had he picked a house with all these damn stairs?

Pulling the bourbon out of the cupboard, he didn't bother with a glass, and took it over to the

French doors, and stared out at the distant city. He took a long pull, and coughed at the intensity of the heady fumes, relishing the burn. The great leveler would soon even things out, help him wind down, unspool all the stress.

Thinking about the evening, he had to smile. That prowl car might not even have been looking for him. Considering he was going to sleep in his own bed tonight, that had gone pretty well.

TWENTY-FOUR

SLATER'S MOUTH FELT DRY when he woke in the morning, but his head didn't hurt. He must not have overindulged. His phone was ringing, he realized, and he scrabbled for it on the bedside table. Conrad. He picked up.

"Pancakes," Conrad said. "Victim states suspect threw pancakes at him."

"What are you talking about?"

"I'm looking at a police report from Central from last night. It has your name all over it."

"How did they get my name?" Slater said. "I didn't give it to anyone."

"The woman who got arrested knew your name, plus anyone who knows you who happened to catch the anonymous assault victim interviewed on channel 6 last night. I didn't see it, but Doris did."

He pulled the phone away from his ear to

glance at the screen. "Yeah, there's a couple messages from her."

"Busted."

"I'm sure your report clearly states that I didn't do anything wrong. And Doris can't bust me. I'm not twelve years old."

"Doris can still kick your ass, and you know it," Conrad said. "What the hell happened?"

"I was the victim of a vicious assault, in a public place, with many objective witnesses."

"By a woman who weighs a buck forty and has a full manicure."

"Those claws draw blood."

"Are you going to take this to court? You'll have to go in and actually make a statement first."

"I don't think I will," Slater said. "Right now my focus really needs to be on healing. My memory of the event is already fading. I think it's my mind protecting me from the trauma, you know? So I'm getting fuzzy on the details."

"You're saying you'd make a poor witness, so nobody will press charges. Why bother calling the cops in the first place?"

"I didn't call anybody," he said flatly. "They were sitting at a table in the pub."

"The paramedic said she thought the blood was mostly pancake syrup."

"She said that? That seems insensitive, coming from a medical professional. I was seriously injured."

"I find that far-fetched," Conrad said. "Whatever you're up to, knock it off. And stop wasting public resources."

"Sir, yes, sir," he said, and hung up on him.

He had to deal with Doris, he knew, studying the screen—she'd just keep calling. He took a breath to steel himself, then dialed, and got into it with her.

———◆———

SOMETIME AFTER SLATER HAD made coffee, and got dressed, Etta rang the bell.

"Where's all the bandages?" she said when he pulled open the door. "There was so much blood on you last night I thought you'd be in the ICU."

"I wanted it to be dramatic," he said, and waved her up the stairs.

"It was plenty dramatic. Mary Louise even showed up. She only comes out for the really good stuff."

"I was thinking about that," Slater said, and paused on the landing at the bedrooms. "She got there too fast. She must have been around already covering something else."

"Mary Louise works in mysterious ways."

"Was it too much blood?"

"It was a lot," Etta said. "That couldn't have been your own."

"I guess I might have overdone it a little. I don't think the paramedic was buying it."

"What the hell were you doing?"

"Do you want a beer? We can sit."

"It's the middle of the day, so no booze," she said. "But I'll take some of that lemonade you had."

Walking up the stairs, he said over his shoulder,

"Beer isn't booze, Etta."

In the kitchen he poured lemonade into a couple of glasses, and they sat outside on the deck, and he told her about the op. Once he'd gone through it, Etta sat back, absorbing it all.

"You're such an asshole."

He waved a hand. "I'm not the one who went to jail. I win."

"You have to admit that stunt was pretty juvenile."

"I don't see it that way at all. Chila tried to get me bogged down in some bureaucratic investigation, even mess up my career, so I paid her back double. She got hoist with her own petard."

"You're the one who did the hoisting," Etta said.

"I'm sure she's home already. Her son would have bailed her out. They're affluent suburbanites."

"It seems so risky. If the first responders had figured out that was fake blood, and you weren't really injured, you'd be the one in jail for trying to frame her."

"It's also risky for them to blame the victim. Chila took a swing at me, and the cops saw that." Slater shrugged. "She earned a night in the hoosegow."

"If you spent a night inside every time you punched someone, you'd still be there."

"I'm smart enough not to do it in front of a bunch of cops. Last night those cops were the victims too. They were already off shift, just chilling and eating their nachos, but they had to step in and deal with Chila's irrational violent outburst."

Etta sat up and drained her glass. "Let's go look at your walls."

They went down to his bedroom, and she walked around the bed, and threw the curtains open wider.

"You're just painting the one room?" Etta said.

"For now."

"And you're going to do it yourself? You know you can hire people."

"I've got the time, now that I'm done with Chila, and Pike's not around. I thought it might be meditative." He waved at the room. "So what color?"

"You get great light," she said. "I'm thinking periwinkle."

"That's blue, right?"

"A bright blue that's leaning toward purple. It'll make the room come alive."

"Can you come with me to the hardware store?"

Etta grinned. "Sure."

She followed the Thunderbird in her little red Prius, and once she'd pored over the paint chips, it didn't take her long to make a selection. Soon Slater had two gallon cans in hand, and rollers and brushes and trays, and said good-bye to Etta in the parking lot.

He almost missed the freeway exit, on autopilot to go back to Westlake. But Westlake was in the past—things were different now. He drove around the end of the lake and into his neighborhood, the route feeling more routine, and spent the afternoon painting his bedroom. Most of the work was in the prep, taking down the drapes and shifting the bed and taping the floor and the ceiling. It was soothing, in a way, rolling the paint on. He liked the smell of it, and the challenge in trying to get it even. It was like a controlled synthetic version of working with plants.

Once he was finished, he carried the tools down to the garage, and chucked the empty paint cans, and washed up in the laundry sink. As he was drying his hands, the doorbell rang.

Pulling open the front door, he found Woody, standing there and grinning at him. He gestured to Slater's T-shirt.

"Are you painting?"

"Not anymore," Slater said. "I just did my bedroom."

"Nice. I like that color."

He looked down and saw that his T-shirt was smeared with the bright periwinkle. "Do you want to come up?"

"I don't have a lot of time, but sure," Woody said. On the landing he paused. "Hold up. I want to see what you did." Stepping into the bedroom, he looked around. "This is great. It feels lived-in now." Across the hall, he stuck his head into the other bedroom. "This one still needs some color. And an actual bed."

"You sound like my mother." Slater led the way up to the kitchen. "Do you want a beer?"

"Hit me," Woody said, and sat at the dining table.

Slater pulled two Coronas from the fridge, and popped them open, and sat with Woody. They clinked the bottle necks together. After he'd taken a sip, Woody spoke.

"So O'Dowd got the ball rolling. We have preliminary approval for the payout."

"Right on. I know she knows what she's doing. And Lindsay Nguyen certainly works fast. I thought it might take months."

"It wasn't her personally," Woody said. "We dealt with her minions. One of them said all the documentation was in order. They wanted to expedite it because it's such a large amount. They're doing a campaign right now to raise public awareness about unclaimed property. I'm going to record a brief interview with the controller as a public service."

"I'd say Lindsay Nguyen is up for reelection."

Woody laughed. "That might be it."

"Don't mention my name when you do that."

"I won't." He reached into his back pocket, and pulled out his wallet, and fished out a slip of paper, handing it to Slater. "I wanted to say thanks."

It was a check, Slater realized, looking it over.

"Thirty grand? Seriously?" He eyed Woody. "You don't have to pay me. O'Dowd did the work."

"She got her fee. Without you I wouldn't have got anything. I feel bad that it's only one percent."

"One percent of that payout is extremely generous."

"This money is about my dad," Woody said. "I was thinking he would have liked you. The no-nonsense thing. He was a bit of a hard-ass himself."

"Well, I won't say no to this," he said, setting

the check on the table. "I've got a mortgage to pay."

Woody didn't linger, and Slater was actually glad that he didn't want to hook up. He never should have slept with him in the first place—he needed to keep his dick out of his cases.

Once he'd rehung the drapes in his bedroom, and pulled down all the masking tape, he changed into a clean shirt for the drive to LAX. Pike was landing soon. He backed the Thunderbird out of the garage and headed toward the freeway.

Accelerating up the ramp and merging into the traffic, Slater couldn't help but grin. It was a good day—he hadn't expected to get paid any more on this job, and he'd been anticipating Pike's arrival since the moment he'd left. Sweet beautiful Pike. Just the thought of him made his stomach hurt, and the sex was primo. As much as he hated to admit it, the sex was actually better because he felt sticky about the guy.

———•———

www.ingramcontent.com/pod-product-compliance
Lightning Source LLC
Chambersburg PA
CBHW010842190726
48286CB00012BA/2953